Maida's Little Hospital

The Maida Books

By INEZ HAYNES IRWIN

>>>->>>->>><-<<<-<<<-<<<

Maida's Little Hospital

BY INEZ HAYNES IRWIN

Grosset & Dunlap

PUBLISHERS

NEW YORK

To

NINA HEIDELBERGER

Granddaughter of My Beloved Friends

NINA AND MICHAEL

Contents

x _Contents_

Maida's Little Hospital

I

Maida and Dicky

A BOY AND GIRL were walking together in the pleasant sunshine of an early spring day. The girl's name was Maida Westabrook, the boy's Dicky Dore.

Maida was a pretty girl. Her eyes—"doves' eyes," as her father sometimes described them—were gay and very gentle in expression. Her hair, which under a light blue beret, fell to her shoulders, was a pale, shining, rippled gold. Gentleness seemed to be the constant expression in her little pointed face. Yet firmness was there and strength. She wore a light-blue coat and light-blue rubber boots.

Dicky was tall and slender, as dark as Maida was fair, with straight brown hair. His look was a happy one. His big dark eyes sparkled continuously and his lips seemed always to be curling into a smile. He wore a woolen coat of a red and yellow plaid, and a red worsted cap with a tassel. Rubber boots came nearly to his knees. The two were walking over the stepping stones which ran between two trees, over the lawn of a charming Cape Cod house, to the road.

"Just think, Maida," Dicky said, "we're going to spend the whole summer in the Little House! Won't that be fun?"

With one impulse they turned and looked back.

The Little House was like hundreds of old houses which dot the countryside of New England. It was two-storied. From the front, a little, windowed, roomlike vestibule made an entrance. All the shingles which covered its roof and sides were old, adzed out long ago by hand. All the tiny panes in its many windows were old too, full of the lines and bubbles of early glass.

"I can't imagine a nicer house," Dicky said.

"I don't believe there is a lovelier one anywhere," Maida agreed.

But like most old houses in New England, the Little House had grown some additions. At one side, a row of sheds which connected it with a great barn had been turned into rooms. On the other, a modern ell extended, several rooms and bathrooms long. At the back, although the two children could not see it, was a big living room which was mostly windows, the exact size of the dining room which, years before, had been the old kitchen.

"I suppose, Maida, you're wondering why I asked you to take a walk with me," Dicky said.

"I *am* wondering," Maida replied smilingly. "But of course I love to take a walk at any time."

"There's something I've wanted to say to you for

a long time, Maida," Dicky went on. "I never seemed to find the chance. But today, when all the rest of the Big Eight went off in the beach wagon and you decided to stay at home, I said to myself, 'Now's the time!'"

"I can't guess what you're going to say, Dicky," Maida said, "but I'm listening. Go on!"

They had turned, and were now crossing the road and, for a moment, Dicky talked of other things. "I love the Little House any time," he said, "but somehow in the spring it seems more—more beautiful than at any other time."

"I never can make up my mind when it's most beautiful," Maida answered. "I love it in the fall, when the leaves turn every color of the rainbow, and I love it in the winter, when everything is so white and sparkling and so covered with snow that nothing is its own real shape, and icicles hang from the eaves and at every wind the trees drop little flurries of snowflakes and—and—oh, so many things happen that I can't think of them all. And I love it in the summer, when all the flowers are in bloom and the sky is such a deep blue and the clouds sometimes are just like mountains of whiteness."

"But now in the spring," Dicky took it up. "Why, look at the snowdrops just coming into bud in the garden, and yet there still are drifts of snow under the bushes. Pretty soon we'll go hunting for mayflowers and the whole house will smell so sweet. And the first thing we know, the roses will be out over the front-door vestibule."

"Yes," Maida agreed, "perhaps spring is the most beautiful season here—except," she added mischievously, "summer, autumn and winter."

"I guess you're right, Maida," Dicky admitted. "All four seasons are the best."

They had passed into the wet, spongy woods across the road. Here was half-cleared land, partially covered with the uncultivated bushes and trees that had always grown there.

"Let's go through the Bosky Dingle and down to the Magic Mirror," Dicky suggested.

The Bosky Dingle was a tree-filled hollow through which the children who lived in the Little House, and who were called the Big Eight, had worn a path. Presently that path came flush against a little pond. About its blue waters the leafless trees had drawn a transparent brown veil. On the beach at one side lay two floats which, in swimming weather, were tethered together several rods apart on the surface of the water.

They walked along the side of the pond. Occasionally Dicky picked up a pebble and scaled it across the surface of the water. But it was evident that he was not thinking of what he was doing. Presently the path led to a long ledge of shale protruding waist high out of the spongy earth.

"Let's sit down on House Rock," Dicky suggested.

They sat down. Bright sunlight streamed over them, but the wind was cold. Dicky buttoned up his reefer and Maida pulled the collar of her coat closer about her.

"Maida," Dicky asked, "do you ever think of Primrose Court?"

"Primrose Court!" Maida exclaimed. "Think about it! I should say I did. I even dream about it. Why, it was there that the Big Six first met."

"Tell me how you happened to go to live in Primrose Court," Dicky said. "I knew once, but I have forgotten."

"It's like a story," Maida declared. "You see, I had been sick for a long time and it looked as though I were going to be lame all my life. Then my father heard of a great doctor in Germany who performed operations on people who were ill just the way I was. Father had him come to America. He performed his famous operation on me. It was successful, but I did not seem to get well. I was never hungry, and I wasn't interested in anything."

"I know just how you felt," Dicky commented. "Remember, I was lame too."

"I remember. Well, one day, we were driving from the house in Pride's Crossing up to the Beacon Street house in Boston. We went through Charlestown. Everyone was talking but me. I wasn't interested in anything. And then suddenly I saw the loveliest little shop on a corner, opposite a big school. Oh, it was such a darling little shop! Do you remember it?"

"Perfectly," Dicky said, grinning.

"It had two windows, one in front beside the door and one at the side, and both windows had toys in them. I told my father that I would like to go into that little shop. So he had the chauffeur stop the car and we all went in. Oh, it was so sweet! There were two showcases on the counter inside, one filled with candies and the other with toys."

"I remember it," Dicky said, his eyes dancing. "Whenever I got a penny, which wasn't very often, I spent it there."

"Well," Maida continued, "somehow my father realized how delighted I was with that little shop. Our doctor had told him that I was perfectly well and that he couldn't do anything more for me. He said that father must find something that would interest me. My father bought the shop and I came to live there with my nurse, Granny Flynn."

"She was my own grandmother," Dicky interrupted, "but I didn't know it then. She was looking everywhere for mother and Delia and me."

"It was just like a storybook," Maida commented solemnly, "the way you found each other. Father had the store painted. He put up a lovely pale-blue sign, with the name in gold letters, Maida's Little Shop. Granny Flynn and I lived in the rooms over the shop. We had a garden. I went with Granny Flynn regularly to Boston and bought new toys and new candies and pickle limes and—oh, everything. And then I began to get acquainted with the children in the neighborhood."

"I was your first friend," Dicky declared proudly.

"You were my first friend," Maida agreed affectionately.

"I was lame then," Dicky added. "I wore a brace

on my leg. I never could play any of the games the other children played."

"You were ill," Maida declared. "I can remember just how you looked the first time I ever saw you. Granny and I talked it over. Your face was thin and your skin was just like putty. Your eyes seemed so big and—yes, they looked sad."

"And then you began to meet the others," Dicky changed the subject.

"Oh yes," Maida went on, "Rosie Brine! I thought Rosie was the most beautiful girl I ever saw in my life with her black, black curls and her black, black eyes and her red, red lips and her red, red cheeks. I used to think that she should have been called Rose Red. Then I met Laura. Laura was so pretty, too, with her blue eyes and her long braids. How I envied her those braids! And then I met Laura's brother, Harold. To tell you the truth I was a little afraid of Laura and Harold. They could do so many things. Laura could dance and play the piano. And Harold was so athletic."

"I used to envy them too," Dicky said. "And today they're just as smart—that isn't the word—as—" Dicky floundered.

"Accomplished," Maida supplied the missing adjective. "That's what father always called them— accomplished."

"But I'm not the least bit envious of them now," Dicky declared.

"I'm not either," Maida agreed. "But that's because

you play the violin so well that you don't have to be envious of what other people can do. And I enjoy their accomplishments so much that I haven't time to be envious."

"Then you met Arthur," Dicky prodded Maida. "What a great boy Arthur is!"

"He certainly is!" Maida agreed again. "There's something about Arthur that— Well, I don't know how to describe it."

"I guess it is that he isn't like anyone else," Dicky decided.

"I guess that's what it is," Maida agreed for the third time, after a silent period in which she thought over Dicky's phrase. "And then I met your mother—"

"I'll never forget the day my mother and my grandmother found each other," Dicky interrupted, taking the words out of Maida's mouth. "Oh, how happy we were! And your father asked your doctor to look me over, and he made me well. Pretty soon I didn't have to wear that brace any more. And your father—"

"My father," Maida continued the story, in her turn taking the words out of Dicky's mouth, "invited all of you to visit me at the Little House. And how it all came about I don't exactly remember, but my father asked all your fathers and mothers if you could stay here, and they said you could. And my father—"

"Your father asked my mother if she'd keep house for you," Dicky interrupted again, "and so we all four came here—mother, Granny, Delia and I."

"And then down here, we met Silva and Tyma Burle—" Maida started again.

"Gypsies!" Dicky again interrupted as though he was afraid that Maida would forget.

"Gypsies," Maida repeated. "They had no one to look after them, and so father invited them to come here. First we were the Big Six. But when Silva and Tyma came to live with us, we became the Big Eight."

"But every summer," Dicky put in, "when your father invites another pair to visit us, for a while we grow into the Big Ten."

"That's the whole story," Maida ended. "And now tell me, why did you want to talk it over with me, Dicky?"

"It's kind of hard to tell why," Dicky answered. "But you see, when I realize that if it hadn't been for your father, I would be dragging a leg all my life, and I might have to be wearing that terrible brace, or carrying a crutch—well, I want to pay it back in some way. I know I can't do anything for Mr. Westabrook. But I can do something for some other lame fellow who is so discouraged he almost wishes he was dead. But somehow when I say it, it seems—" Dicky looked downcast.

"Go on, Dicky," Maida urged in a voice sharp for her. "I'm very, very much interested."

"Well, I thought since you'd been lame, too, you might feel the same way I did. I thought that, as your father always invites two other children to stay with us during the summer, we might ask if, this year, they could be a little lame boy and a little lame girl. Then you and I might be able to pay back to two other sick children what's been done for us."

Dicky paused and looked at Maida—a strange look that was part inquiring and part beseeching. "Do you think it's crazy, Maida?" he demanded.

For a moment, Maida did not speak. Embarrassed, Dicky started to get up. "Dicky," Maida said in a tone that stopped him like a bullet. "Dicky, I think it's the loveliest plan I ever heard in my life. And I'm ashamed—dreadfully ashamed—that I did not think of it myself. We'll ask my father about it tonight. But Dicky," Maida continued, "let's not tell the rest of the Big Eight about this until we talk with my father and Bunny and Robin Hood."

"Of course not!" Dicky answered.

Then as with one impulse, "There comes the beach wagon!" he and Maida exclaimed together.

They slid hastily down the rough side of the ledge of rock.

Suddenly Maida stopped short. "What's that that sparkles so?" she exclaimed.

On the ground, just where the rock pulled up from the earth, the sunlight caught on something and then flashed away from it in color. Both children bent swiftly to it. Their heads knocked together. They laughed as they straightened themselves up. But Maida had picked up the tiny glittering object. She rolled it between her fingers to get the dried earth off. Then she held it out to Dicky on the palm of her hand.

"It's my little crystal ball!" she exclaimed. "I lost it long ago. I must have left it out here when I was playing house. It stayed out all winter long. It must have worked deep into the ground and now it's worked out again."

"It's beautiful," Dicky said admiringly. He held it up to the light, squinting at it. "I've read that some people can tell fortunes by crystal balls."

"Let's see if we can read our fortunes in it," Maida suggested, giggling. "Are we going to have a little lame boy and a little lame girl visit us?" she asked it.

Still giggling, Maida and Dicky peered into the tiny crystal, but all they could see was the blue sky reflected in it and the sparkle that the sun brought to it.

II

Mr. Westabrook and the Big Eight

A MUCH-USED beach wagon had just stopped on the road in front of the Little House, and a group of boys and girls—the rest of the Big Eight—were leaping out of it. The boys all wore worsted caps, coats plaided in brilliant squares, and rubber boots that came nearly to their knees. The girls wore bright scarves on their heads, coats that came below their knees, and slacks that disappeared into rubber boots; red or white or orange in color.

On the front seat sat a young man and a young woman. The man, tall and broad-shouldered, muscular and strong-looking, black-haired, blue-eyed, was the greatest possible contrast to the young woman. She was little and slender and brown, full of curves, curls, dimples, smiles and laughter. They were Mr. and Mrs. Robert Hood, who lived with the Big Eight in the Little House as their teachers and playmates.

The Big Eight called Mrs. Hood Bunny. They called Mr. Hood Robin.

Maida addressed herself to Mrs. Hood. "Bunny," she said, "may I call up my father and ask him to come over here tonight?"

"Of course, Maida," Bunny answered. She studied Maida's excited face. "Is it anything important? Has something happened?"

"Nothing has happened, Bunny dear," Maida replied. "But it is important."

"Ask him if he'd like to come to supper," Bunny suggested.

"Let me know, Maida," Rosie Brine said, "if your father decides to come to supper. I'll bake some apples for him."

Rosie Brine, with her flashing black eyes, her shining black hair, her redly blooming cheeks and lips, might still have borne the name that Maida had given her before she knew her—Rose Red.

"I'll telephone right away," Maida assured her.

"What do you suppose Dicky and I have been talking about?" Maida asked the home-comers. But before they could reply, she answered her own question. "Primrose Court."

"Primrose Court," Silva Burle repeated. "I always feel a little jealous whenever you talk of Primrose Court, because Tyma and I didn't know you then."

It was plain that Silva never really had entertained so bitter a feeling as jealousy—her expression was too sweet. Her coloring was as delicate as Rose's was decided. Soft were her amber eyes, soft her leaf-brown, short hair, soft as the petals of a tearose, and as delicately tinted, her complexion. "But I don't think you ever feel jealous, Tyma." She turned to her brother.

Tyma Burle was a striking-looking lad with jet-black, close-waved hair and big brilliant eyes of purple-blue. "I often think," he admitted, "of the fun you must have had in Primrose Court and with Maida's Little Shop. And yet, I learned a lot about the woods and birds and animals all those years that Silva and I moved from place to place, living in tents. I wouldn't like to give that up. I'd like to have had both. But I guess you can't have everything."

"Never was truer word spoken," Robin Hood approved. "Sometimes I think life is made up of choosing. And all you can do is to make the wisest decision you can when the choice comes."

"I'd much prefer Tyma's woods," Arthur Duncan declared.

Arthur was the biggest and strongest of all the boys. The least handsome of them all, he had, in his steady, heavily fringed gray eyes and his strong, big features, a look of power.

Arthur paused and thought for a moment. "That is, if I hadn't made such good friends at Primrose Court. A fellow can't give up his friends. It's very puzzling." Arthur scowled and abandoned his problem.

"I guess we'd all take the friends," Harold Lathrop declared.

Harold, standing close beside Arthur, presented

the greatest possible contrast to him. Blue-eyed, fair-haired, slender, quick as a cat, Harold was like a thin, swift silver sword; and Arthur was like a heavy, strong iron spear.

Laura, Harold's sister, flashed a gay smile at her brother, a smile that made her blue-eyed, delicately pretty face even prettier. "I certainly would," she said. "I'm glad I lived in Primrose Court. I'm glad I made all these friends there. I'm glad I met Maida. I'm glad we're all living together in the Little House and I hope to goodness that we never grow up and that we live here for hundreds of thousands of years."

The Big Eight greeted Laura's outburst of affectionate eloquence with applause, and then they all poured into the Little House.

Maida went at once to the telephone.

The Westabrook estate was a huge tract of land bordering Massachusetts Bay. The Little House was the original Westabrook house, nearly three hundred years old. In it lived the Big Eight. Mr. Westabrook lived in the Big House, some distance away. From there he could keep in constant communication with his little motherless daughter and yet entertain easily his hosts of friends. It happened that he was at home today. He came immediately to the telephone at Maida's call.

"Father," Maida said, "something very important has come up, and we want to talk it over with you. It's not anything worrying," she hastened to reassure him. "It's something so exciting—you've got to know about it at once. I mean I've got to talk about it with you at once. Could you come over to the Little House this evening? Come to supper, father. Rosie is waiting to hear if you will. She wants to bake some apples for you."

Mr. Westabrook laughed his deep roar. "Of course I'll come. I'd break any engagement for those baked apples. I'll be there late in the afternoon."

An immediate bustle and hustle set up in the Little House. Rosie retired to the kitchen, from which delicious smells soon began to waft. Maida, assisted by Silva, put more leaves in the big dining-room table and set it for eleven; Laura went out into the garden and picked a big bunch of green leaves, snowdrops, and crocuses, purple and yellow. She arranged them in a low bowl and put them in the center of the table. Then all four tidied up the big living room, where the books and magazines of the day's reading lay helter-skelter, here and there.

Presently Mr. Westabrook came striding into the house. Before he could take his coat and hat off, he was the center of the milling Big Eight, the boys shaking the hand nearest them and the girls battling for hugs.

Jerome Westabrook was always called "Buffalo" Westabrook by the newspapers. That was because, having, like Abraham Lincoln, been a rail-splitter in his youth, a great development of muscle between his shoulders seemed to push his powerful, shaggy-haired head forward and make it seem even more powerful. His dark eyes, with their sharp, steel-steady, examining look, frightened strangers. But those eyes could be both kind and gay.

Mr. Westabrook brought into the house an atmosphere so keen and exciting that it was always as though a cold, clear north wind had blown through the place. Immediately all the other occupants hurried down to the living room. Besides Robin and Bunny, there were Granny Flynn and Mrs. Dore, Dicky's grandmother and mother.

Granny Flynn always donned her best gown, a black silk, when Mr. Westabrook appeared. And tonight she put in her high-piled, silvery hair a big silver comb which Mr. Westabrook had given her.

"You look more than ever like a fairy godmother, Granny Flynn," Mr. Westabrook said to Maida's beloved old nurse, "but tonight you are a very elegant one."

Granny Flynn's answer to this was to sweep a deep curtsy to Mr. Westabrook, to which he responded with a very elegant bow from the waist.

Mrs. Dore looked very handsome in a pale cream-colored dress, with a pair of brilliant red earrings that made her eyes more sparkling.

The delicious supper consisted of one of Florabel's huge, high omelets, a big mixed salad, hot biscuits and—

"Oh, don't they look good!" Mr. Westabrook exclaimed when Poppy appeared carrying a big platter of Rosie's baked apples. "I know I'm going to turn at once into Mr. Pig."

Mr. Westabrook did indeed eat three of the baked apples. He looked longingly at a fourth, but, "No, I guess I'd better not," he decided sadly.

After Mr. Westabrook had drunk the last drop of his black coffee, they all went into the living room where Zeke, the colored man, was just putting a match to the fire that Arthur had laid. The flames leaped high, turned into huge golden oak leaves and tore at the piled logs.

Everybody found seats, the Big Eight obviously bursting with something they wanted to say. Mr. Westabrook took a cigar from his case. Robin filled his pipe and lighted it.

"Now," Mr. Westabrook said, "what is all this about?"

Maida made Dicky tell her father of his plan.

Mr. Westabrook, puffing busily, listened without a change of expression. He did not speak for a moment, when Dicky finished, and Dicky's look turned downcast.

Suddenly Mr. Westabrook spoke. "I'm ashamed that I did not think of that myself, Dicky. It's a beautiful plan, and we'll manage to carry it out some way or other."

Dicky's face was all light and happiness again. "But Mr. Westabrook," he said, a little falteringly, "I don't want you to do it all. I want to help in some way. I've saved up my allowance for a long time now, and I'd like to give that toward the expense of it. And I'd come to the Big House as many afternoons as you needed me and work on the place."

Mr. Westabrook's expression did not change. "We'll talk about that later," he pronounced. "How do the rest of you feel about this plan, Big Eight?" he asked.

Rosie, as usual, spoke first. "I'm wild about it!" she declared, all sparkles of black eyes and pearly teeth. "And I hope they'll be a boy and a girl, Mr. Westabrook," she added, "because the boys can look after the lame boy, and we girls can look after the lame girl."

"It must be a boy and a girl," Mr. Westabrook approved.

"Rosie'll cook such delicious things for them to eat," Laura sighed. "Silva'll paint pictures for them, and Maida, who's such a wonderful nurse, will take care of them. I want to do something too—but I can't think of anything," she finished mournfully.

"I can," Silva declared. "You can knit them each a pair of socks, Laura. Don't you remember how you used to knit when we first came here?"

"Yes, I can," Laura exclaimed in a delighted voice. "I'll order some yarn the moment they come. I want to see what color the girl's eyes are first. I suppose the boy won't mind what color his socks are."

"Now we'll hear from the boys," Mr. Westabrook said, pressing out the lighted end of his cigar against an ashtray and immediately lighting another.

"I think it will be great," Arthur approved. "I always like it when other boys and girls come here. They've all been so much fun."

"Perhaps the boy will play some instrument,"

Dicky said hopefully. "Why, then, with my violin we'll have an orchestra!"

Everyone laughed. "Perhaps he'll be a stamp collector," Harold suggested, "like me."

"Or a woodsman," put in Tyma, "like me."

"I've left you to the last, Bunny and Robin," Mr. Westabrook said, "but only because what you say is very important. How about it?"

"I can't think of anything better for the Big Eight," Bunny declared. She was all smiles and dimples, yet underneath lay seriousness.

"It is what they most need," Robin agreed with his wife. "If anything, Big Eight," he concluded, smiling quizzically, "you have things a little too easy."

"I guess you're right, Robin," Arthur said thoughtfully.

In a swift, loud enthusiastic burst of assent, the Big Eight agreed.

"Father," Maida asked suddenly, "do you remember the crystal ball you gave me years ago and how I lost it and how heartbroken I was?"

"I do remember it," Mr. Westabrook answered.

"You can scarcely believe this, father," Maida went on, "but I found it today, near House Rock, where I used to play with dolls. Dicky was there and he said some people can tell fortunes by looking in crystal balls. We both tried to find something in it, but we couldn't. You try to see something, please!"

Maida took the crystal ball from her pocket and handed it to Mr. Westabrook. He studied it carefully under the light. "I see a lot of things," he said finally, "and among them two children, a boy and a girl, who are coming to the Little House. What a pity! They're both lame. Their faces are turned away, so I can't see what they look like."

"Father, you darling fraud!" Maida exclaimed, throwing her arms about Mr. Westabrook's neck. "You don't see them at all. But you will!" she declared, "and we'll take such good care of them!"

"Maida's Little Hospital!" Dicky exclaimed.

"*Our* Little Hospital!" Maida corrected him firmly.

III

Scrab and Midge

A FEW WEEKS later came a day when excitement burst out all over the Little House. Early in the morning Robin Hood and Bunny started for Boston in the beach wagon. The moment they were gone, everybody fell to swift, intense and concentrated work.

Granny Flynn and Mrs. Dore, it is true, went about their usual tasks, Granny dusted the nursery where two very little girls—Delia, Dicky's sister, and Nesta, Silva and Tyma's sister—were playing with blocks. Then she dusted her own room and her daughter's. Her movements were birdlike in their swiftness and accuracy. And as she worked, she crooned "The Wearing of the Green." Mrs. Dore, taking Bunny's long list of provisions, departed in the convertible with Zeke and Florabel to do the marketing.

The four girls mopped and dusted their rooms, and put fresh towels in the bathrooms. An extra bed had been placed in Maida's room. The desk had been moved out and a second bureau put in its place. A mirror hung over it. On the bureau Maida placed a comb, a brush and a hand mirror of pearl-white plastic and, under the mirror, a bowlful of spring flowers —narcissi, daffodils, violets and tulips. On the bookshelf she ranged her favorite books, *At the Back of the North Wind; Curdie and the Goblin; The Princess and Curdie; Little Women; An Old-Fashioned Girl.*

"It looks perfectly sweet here," she called to the other girls, who were working with equal swiftness in their own rooms.

"Wait till you see mine!" Laura exclaimed. "I've brushed up with a toothbrush."

"I'm using my manicure set," Rosie sang out.

"I'm dusting with a lace handkerchief," Silva declared, "with perfume on it."

In the meantime, the boys, who had moved into their summer quarters in the barn, were working too, perhaps not quite so conscientiously, but with a good deal of slap-dash movement. At any rate, the upper floor of the barn, where they slept, looked shipshape with its four carefully made beds, one to a corner, each with a bureau beside it, bearing a pair of hairbrushes, a comb and a mirror, and a chair set straight against the wall beside each bureau.

"All this work is wasted, in a way," Arthur growled suddenly. "If the lame boy is still using a wheelchair and if he's going to sleep in the New Ell, it will be a long time before he gets up these stairs to this room."

"I never thought of that," Dicky said. After a moment's thought, "Let's put the dust all back," he suggested cheerfully.

"We'll have to do it all over the day he does move in here," Tyma said dolefully.

"You fellows talk as if you'd done a day's work," said Harold, who was much the most orderly and efficient among them. "I think we could do this all over again without breaking down."

The other three boys laughed. "I don't mind making a bed," Arthur admitted, "but, oh, how I hate to dust!"

Presently the girls attacked the living room and the dining room, the boys the Map room and the Book Room.

"Oh dear," Laura said later, "how I hate to wait!"

The girls, in fresh slacks and blouses, the boys, with faces unnaturally clean and hair so slicked down that it looked like satin, had assembled in the living room.

"Goodness!" Rosie exclaimed, consulting the clock. "There isn't a thing left to clean. What shall we do until they arrive? If we walk from here to the door, we'll manage someway or other to get all mussed up again. Let's play Buzz. We can play that sitting down."

Buzz was indeed a simple game. Everybody counted, in turn, from one on up indefinitely. But whenever they came to a number with a seven in it, like seven, seventeen, twenty-seven, or a multiple of seven, like fourteen, twenty-one and twenty-eight, they had to substitute the word *Buzz* for that number. Anyone who failed to do this was out of the game. Rosie, who was hopeless in arithmetic, was the first to leave. Dicky, who could never remember that seven times eight was fifty-six, went down next. Then came Tyma, Maida and Laura. Harold, Silva and Arthur battled it out alone until Harold finally won.

The defeated ones clamored for another chance at Buzz, and this time Maida won. After that, they decided to sing. Rounds entertained them most, so that, over and over again, they produced "Three Blind Mice" and "Scotland's Burning." Suddenly between verses, Tyma, who had the keenest hearing among them, cocked a listening ear toward the window. "The beach wagon!" he exclaimed.

The Big Eight rushed to the door.

Yes, the beach wagon was approaching. The noise of the wheels grew louder and louder. Suddenly the car came into sight, swept up the road and stopped in front of the Little House. Robin leaped out and gave his hand to Bunny. Zeke appeared from the kitchen.

The back seats had been taken out of the beach wagon. Side by side, two wheelchairs rested where the seats had been. In one sat a little girl, carefully buttoned up in a long, loose coat of an ugly brown. A faded brown felt hat rested on her head. She could have been, not so much a pretty as a picturesque, child. Her hair, of so deep a red that it was almost wine color, fluttered about her face in flying ringlets.

Her excited, long-lashed eyes were brown—too big for her pale, peaked face. A crutch rested against her knee.

"Big Eight," Bunny said, "this is one of your guests, Midge Golightly." As the Big Eight stepped forward to shake hands with the little lame girl, Bunny gave their names.

"I think I could pick you out," Midge said shyly. "Mrs. Hood—Bunny, she told me to call her—described you all so carefully." She smiled, and suddenly the little pointed face, lighted by its wistful smile, was so pathetic that Maida, as she confessed afterwards to the girls of the Big Eight, had to swallow a lump in her throat.

"And this young man," Bunny went on pleasantly, as Robin and Zeke lifted the second wheelchair onto the ground, "is Scrab Morgan." And again, as the Big Eight stepped forward to shake hands with their second guest, she called them by name.

Scrab Morgan was thin too, much thinner than Midge. He looked as though the skin of his flesh had been pulled tight over his skull. But out of that pallid mask gleamed a pair of eyes that were like green ice, so clear were they, and so cold.

Scrab Morgan wore a dirty coat which looked as though it had been cut down to fit him. It was open, displaying faded dungarees. He wore a linen cap with a projecting visor.

Apparently Scrab did not see the outstretched hands of the Big Eight. He did not extend his own. "Hullo!" he said. His voice was as freezing as his eyes.

They wheeled the two invalids to their quarters. Midge, it appeared, could walk upstairs, if she proceeded slowly and used her crutches. Carefully, she climbed the narrow, steep staircase which always, just opposite the front door in old New England houses, leads to the second story. Maida preceded her and the other three girls, in single file, followed her.

"You see, Midge," Rosie explained, "if you happen to stumble, you'd fall into my arms, I'd fall into Silva's and Silva'd fall into Laura's. But using her gigantic strength, Laura would hold on tight to the banisters."

"Just like a pack of cards!" Midge commented gaily.

"Then I," Maida took up their fable, "would pull you back onto your feet, Midge. You'd pull Rosie onto her feet. Rosie'd pull Silva onto her feet. And Silva'd pull Laura onto her feet."

"Let's try it!" Midge suggested. And suddenly she laughed—a laugh as clear and gay as the little sprinkle of notes that the robin drops in the spring.

That night, talking together, the girls of the Big Eight agreed that they liked Midge from the instant she was game enough to suggest all falling downstairs.

"Now, you lie down on the bed for a while, Midge," Maida ordered, the instant they entered their room. She took off Midge's worn coat and her faded hat. And, as Zeke appeared with a soiled, shabby suitcase, she asked, "May I unpack your things and put them away?"

Midge flushed painfully. She started to speak and then swallowed before she could find voice. "My clothes aren't very pretty," she said in a low voice, "but they're all mended up."

Maida opened the suitcase, talking busily all the time. She made no comment on the faded, mended, scrupulously clean dresses and underwear, or on the stockings, so darned that, in the feet, little of the original material showed. She placed the dresses on hangers and put them on the pole in the closet. She piled the few pieces of underwear in the drawers. With them she put the pathetic comb, of which several of the teeth were missing, and the hairbrush, the bristles of which were flattened from long use.

"Probably Bunny will insist, Midge," Maida explained, "that you wear slacks and sweaters like the rest of us. They aren't the least bit like a uniform, but she gets them for all of us. I hope you won't mind."

"Mind!" Midge exclaimed. "I shall love it! I have never had slacks in my life, nor a really pretty sweater."

"You and I are about the same size," Maida suggested. "There's a pair of slacks that I've never had on and a sweater that's just come back from the cleaners. Can I dress you up for dinner?"

Midge turned her face away for a moment. When she turned it back, Maida saw that her eyes were wet. "I can't wait! And thank you, Maida, very, very, *very* much!"

In the meantime, followed by the boys of the Big Eight, Zeke had wheeled Scrab Morgan into the pleasant room on the first floor of the New Ell, a room with its own bathroom, which Scrab was to occupy alone. From that room, he could be wheeled into the main house, or onto the grounds, without going down any stairs. Zeke stopped the chair beside the bed. Then he left the room and returned with a suitcase. Midge's suitcase had been shabby enough, but Scrab's, of a faded, cracked artificial leather, was bursting at the seams. The lock had long ago gone. The bag was tied together with rope.

Scrab looked about the room. The floor was of polished wood, a thick green rug covering the center. At the two windows hung draperies patterned with snow-white callas and green leaves. There was a bureau, a chiffonier, a desk, two comfortable big chairs with slipcovers that matched the curtains, and two straight chairs.

"Pretty ritzy!" Scrab commented.

There was a tone in his voice that Arthur found himself, for exactly what reason he could not discover, resenting, and resenting hotly. He threw wide open the door of the bathroom. Chromium flashed and tiles glittered. The wallpaper showed mermaids and mermen floating underwater among great shells and corals. He opened the door to the closet, empty, but for a bathrobe hanging on the door and files of hangers on the pole which ran down the middle.

"I think you'll like it here," Arthur said, and try as hard as he would, he could not keep the sarcasm out of his voice. "We boys live in the top floor of the barn during the summer. It's not so—ritzy—as this. Tomorrow," he went on, suddenly feeling ashamed of himself, "we'll take you into the lower floor of the barn. That's a swell place. It's a gymnasium. And before you know it, you'll be walking up the stairs to our quarters."

"I shall never walk again," Scrab declared in a voice as hard as iron.

"Oh, say, fellow," Arthur remonstrated, "don't talk like that! Of course you'll walk again and much sooner than you expect."

"Think so?" Scrab asked. And now there was a decided sneer in his voice.

"Yes," Arthur was beginning a little hotly, "I think so," when Dicky interrupted.

"I was just as lame once as you are, Scrab," he explained. "Then Mr. Westabrook sent a doctor to me who cured me. I didn't think I would ever walk again either. But I did, and now I would never know I had ever been lame."

"I'll never walk again," Scrab repeated. His tone was contemptuous, as of one who knew all about the subject under discussion and did not wish to listen to argument.

Harold changed the subject. "Can we unpack for you, Scrab?" he asked.

Scrab did not answer directly. He put his icy gaze on Harold with a long, intent stare. But it was not as though he saw Harold. Obviously he was turning something over in his mind. "Put my suitcase on that!" he ordered, pointing to the straight-backed

chair nearest him. "Don't cut the rope. Untie it! I'll
need the rope when I go back to—to—to wherever
I'm going. Then take the things out in the order in
which I tell you, and put them—put them—well, put
them anywhere!"

In silence, Harold followed Scrab's orders. The
other three boys stood about the room—in silence
too, the silence of shock.

Working swiftly and expertly, Harold untied the
knots in the rope, rolled it, tied the ends, put it in a
corner of the suitcase tray. Then he threw open the
sagging, wrinkled broken top of the suitcase.

The first thing that met his eyes was a parcel
wrapped in newspaper and tied by a cord.

"That package there," Scrab ordered, "the one
with the newspaper around it. Put that in the top
drawer! And don't open it!"

Harold turned on him in a flash. "I don't open
parcels not meant for me!" he said, in a voice as icy as
Scrab's.

"Okay! I'm glad to hear it! Put the parcel in the
top drawer! Put the other things anywhere! I don't
care where they go!"

Midge's few poor belongings had been neatly
packed, but Scrab's were a nest of confusion. Harold
drew out underwear riddled with slits, stockings with
great holes in the heels, a second suit as soiled and
shabby as the one he was wearing, two greasy ties.
Without comment, Harold stacked the underwear
in the chiffonier drawers, hung the suit, the worn
overcoat and the ties in the closet.

"Well, I guess that's all," Scrab commented. Then as though suddenly remembering, he dropped a "Thanks!" He added, "When do we get some chow?"

Dicky answered, "We have dinner at noon, supper at night. There's a buzzer in this room that will wake you for breakfast."

"Service—what!" Scrab exclaimed complacently. "I'll say you're ritzy!"

There was a brief awkward pause. Arthur broke the silence. "What would you like to do now, Scrab?"

"Well, every morning and afternoon, I have to lie down. I generally read until I fall asleep. If one of you guys will help me out of this chair, I'll lie on the outside of the bed. Got anything to read, any of you?"

"We have a whole roomful of books," Arthur answered stiffly. "What do you like to read?"

"Anything that's got murder and shooting or spies and counterspies in it," Scrab replied.

Arthur left the room. When he came back, his arms were full of books. He arranged them on the reading table beside the bed. "We haven't any books about murders. But we have some great adventure stories. Know anything about whaling or lion hunting?"

"No," said Scrab, "but I guess I'd be interested in them."

"Here's *The Cruise of the Cachalot* and here's *Lions in the Way*," Arthur informed him. "I guess if you begin either of them, you won't want to put them down until you've finished them."

Arthur and Tyma eased Scrab from his chair onto the bed.

'So long, fellows!" Scrab called condescendingly as the boys filed out.

No one of the four boys spoke a word. But as by a homing instinct, they made for their big room in the barn. Arthur closed the door after them. He looked hard at the others. "Gee!" he exclaimed.

And—as though helpless in the face of a mystery they could not explain—the other boys also said, "Gee!"

IV

The Guests and the Big Eight

Before dinner, Bunny, followed by Poppy, both with their arms full of brown-paper parcels—entered Midge's room. They deposited their parcels on the bed. Poppy departed. Bunny opened the boxes, filled half the capacious closet with the new clothes that came out of them; completely filled two drawers of the capacious dresser with new underwear and sweaters. On the dresser top, she placed a toilet set in pink plastic—a comb, a brush, a mirror, a tray and several boxes. She repacked the clothes that Midge had brought with her in the old suitcase and stored it away in the attic.

In the meantime, Robin Hood, followed by Zeke, also laden with brown-paper boxes and parcels, noiselessly entered Scrab's room. Both men deposited their packages in the bathroom. Zeke departed. Robin opened the boxes and hung part of their contents in the closet. He had just opened the top drawer of the chiffonier when, having finished his sleep, Scrab woke up. His lids lifted with sleepy slowness at first and then flashed wide open. His eyes were emerald green, lighted with a burning rage.

"Don't you open that parcel!" he screamed. "It's none of your business what's in it!" He kept on hysterically screaming, "Don't you open that package!"

Robin sat down on the bed. He looked Scrab squarely in the eye for a moment. Under his steady gaze, Scrab's screams ran down to a frightened silence.

"I had no intention of opening it, Scrab," Robin declared finally in a quiet voice. "Everyone in the Little House respects everyone else's privacy. We have few rules, but that's one of our most important ones. While we were in Boston, Bunny and I bought some new clothes for you. I wanted to put them away before you awakened. I wanted to surprise you."

Robin arose and opened the door of the closet. Three suits, two windbreakers, one in a blue and green plaid, the other in navy blue and white, dungarees, two cardigan sweaters hung there. Two woolen caps in colors that matched the windbreakers lay on the shelf. On the floor was a tall pair of rubber boots, a pair of sneakers and two pairs of shoes.

Scrab's eyes passed unseeingly over this array. For suddenly he had become calm—and curious. "How come you could do all this without making noise enough to wake me up?"

Robin sat down on the bed again. "Scrab," he said in his friendliest voice, "I'm glad that you are more interested in the answer to that question than in examining your new clothes. You see, I've hunted wild animals on several continents—grizzly in the West of the United States, jaguar in South America, lions, elephant, rhinos and leopards—oh, I can't enumerate them all now—in Africa. I've had to learn to move through thick jungle without making a sound."

Scrab stared at him. "Well. What do you know!" he exclaimed. And then, "Are all those glad rags mine?"

"You betcha, boy!" Robin answered, smiling his most engaging smile.

"Can I put some of them on before dinner?" Scrab asked.

"That's what they're here for," Robin informed him.

"What do you know!" Scrab exclaimed again.

He watched closely but in silence as Robin piled underwear in the chiffonier drawers; put a pair of black military brushes and a hand mirror on the chiffonier top, hung a half dozen ties on the slender metal rod attached to the inside of the closet door. Last of all, Robin repacked Scrab's own clothes in his suitcase, tied it with the rope in the tray and took it upstairs to the attic.

"Now, boy," Robin said on his return, "you're going to have a bath, and then I'll help you into some of those new clothes."

Robin turned on both the hot and cold water faucets in the bathtub. The thunder of the water filled the room.

Over the roaring sound, Scrab screamed, "I can't walk to that bathtub."

Robin turned the water off for a second. "I'll carry you to the tub," he said quietly.

Scrab did not speak again, but when after helping him undress, Robin took him gently in his arms, Scrab smiled. "Did you ever have to carry a dead elephant?" he asked in a voice carefully low.

The hot bath apparently relaxed and relieved some strange mental knot in Scrab's mind. He smiled at his reflection in the glass when, upheld by Robin, he saw himself in dark gray trousers, dark blue socks and a dark blue cardigan sweater. He opened the top drawer of the chiffonier to get a handkerchief. His gaze fell on the newspaper parcel there, and suddenly a look of such tragic misery swept across the young face that Robin turned aside. He did not want Scrab to suspect that he had seen it.

"All ready, fellow?" Robin asked.

Scrab's eyes had turned to ice again. "All set, mister," he replied.

"Please call me Robin," Robin asked gently.

In the meantime, Midge, hopping about on her crutches, made a tiny tour of inspection of the place. The girls showed her House Rock, the Fairy Ring, the Bosky Dingle and the Magic Mirror. When they returned, a faint color had warmed her leaden cheeks. And when she found stretched out on her bed a pair of light-gray slacks and a geranium-pink sweater, her color deepened.

"They're for you, Midge," Maida said. "See!" She opened the closet door. There, half-filling the pole, hung a row of new clothes.

"Oh!" Midge exclaimed, and "Oh!" and "*Oh!*" Like a little lame bird, she hopped over to the closet and stared in, her big eyes radiant. "I never thought I would ever own clothes like these! And are those toilet things meant for me to use?"

"Certainly, and look here!" Maida continued triumphantly. She opened the drawers to Midge's bureau. There lay stacks of underwear, a pile of stockings.

"Maida," Midge asked radiantly, "would it be all right if I put on these clothes right away?"

"Why not?" Maida answered cheerfully.

It was a pair of children quite different from the two who had arrived that morning who came into the dining room at noon.

Maida had pinned a geranium blossom, the exact pink shade of the new sweater, in Midge's red hair. Robin had put a yellow crocus in Scrab's buttonhole. Immediately Midge went up to Bunny and thanked her for her new clothes. But Scrab said nothing. His eyes had turned to ice again and ice they remained all through the meal. He answered Granny's questions or Mrs. Dore's questions with a cool yes'm or no'm. But he added nothing. Midge, however, replied at length, although every few minutes she said, "I guess I'm talking too much. I don't mean to be impolite, but I'm so excited, I just can't seem to stop."

Granny answered, "Of course, the dear choild is excited-loike!" Mrs. Dore said, "Talk all you want, Midge!"

The afternoon passed like many afternoons in the Little House. Yet there was a difference. But, at first, it seemed that it was going to be like all the rest. Arthur wheeled Scrab over to the barn to show him the gymnasium which took up the whole lower floor. Scrab's icy gaze traveled over the athletic fittings, one after another. "Quite a swell joint!" he commented after a while. "Who boxes?"

"We all do," Arthur answered, "but Tyma and I most of all."

"If I was ever going to get well, I'd put the gloves on with you," Scrab returned.

"So you box?" Dicky commented.

"Boxing is where I live," Scrab said. "My uncle Ed—" He stopped suddenly and a look of anguish swept over his face. "My Uncle Ed is a welter, and he trained me. He said he was going to make a pro of me."

The boys stared at him with a new respect.

"Who fences?" Scrab asked.

"Dicky and I," Harold answered.

"You could teach me," Scrab answered, "if I was ever going to get well. Canoes," he commented, looking at the back of the gym, where four canoes were neatly stacked. "Traveling rings, football and baseball outfits, hockey sticks. Say, you fellows have it pretty soft. Who taught you to use all this stuff?"

"Robin Hood," Harold answered. "He knows how to do everything."

"Some guy!" Scrab commented. For the first time there was a note of admiration in his voice.

The boys could not push Scrab's chair through the Bosky Dingle, so it was impossible to show him House Rock, the Fairy Ring and the Magic Mirror.

"To tell you the truth," Arthur said afterwards, "I was glad. I knew he'd only laugh and sneer at them."

But taking turns, the boys wheeled the invalid for a long distance up the road and back. Scrab accepted all this service complacently, without thanks, as though it was his right.

When they got back to the Little House, they found everyone sitting on the lawn. Zeke had brought out a pair of fiber rugs on which he placed big comfortable porch chairs for Granny, Mrs. Dore and Bunny. Beside Bunny was a table spread with bottles of ginger ale, glasses, and plates of cookies. The four girls of the Big Eight sat on the grass. A little distance away, the two babies, Delia and Nesta, played with dolls, stuffed rabbits, elephants, Teddy bears.

"As this is a kind of special day," Bunny greeted them, "I thought we'd have a little celebration."

Robin began to snap off the bottle caps and pour out the ginger ale. The girls passed the glasses and served Midge and Scrab first after the grownups.

"Gee," Scrab approved, but in a voice that still held a note of condescension, "this tastes swell!" He smacked his lips with loud resounding smacks.

And then a strange thing happened.

At the sound of Scrab's voice, Delia looked up and stared at him. Then she scrambled to her feet and—her blue eyes shining and all her thick red curls bobbing—ran as fast as her short legs could carry her, to Scrab's side. She lifted her arms up high. "Take up!" she demanded. This was the phrase she always used when she wanted to be lifted.

Scrab did not hesitate. Instantly, with great gentleness and skill, he lifted the little girl into his lap. Delia snuggled against him, pressed her cheek against Scrab's cheek. "What her name?" she asked.

Everyone was *her* to Delia.

"Scrab," Scrab answered in a voice that none of them had heard from him before.

"Sab," Delia repeated.

"Name's Delia," she informed him. "I love Sab," she announced.

Scrab said nothing.

After a while, Mrs. Dore, thinking that Scrab might find the plump little girl too much of a burden, came forward to lift her off his lap. Delia only clung the closer. "Delia stay, Sab," she begged.

"Don't you find her too heavy, Scrab?" Mrs. Dore asked.

"No'm. I'm used to children," Scrab answered.

His eyes, Maida noticed, were as soft now as melted emeralds. But when they all got up to go into the house, those emeralds had hardened to ice again.

V

Scrab and Arthur and Tyma

THE NEXT DAY was rainy. As though drawn by a fascination they could not resist, the boys, wheeling Scrab, made at once for the gym. But arriving there, the boys of the Big Eight stood about awkwardly for a moment. Somehow they did not wish to engage in any athletic activities with Scrab sitting helpless in his wheelchair.

It was Scrab himself who put an end to this situation. He addressed himself to Arthur. "Why don't you and Tyma put on the gloves? I'd like to see you box!"

"All right!" Tyma agreed. "But I'm not as fast as Arthur."

"Don't expect any fancy footwork from us," Arthur warned him too. "We're not very good."

Arthur and Tyma boxed a great deal together and always in the best of humor. Robin had worked hard to instill in the Big Eight the spirit of sportsmanship and the principle of fair play. Tyma and Arthur always commended each other's punches.

Today the boys put on their gloves, took positions on the mat and squared off. Harold held a stop watch to time the rounds. Gradually Harold and Dicky froze into a horrified silence. For, from the beginning, it was as though Scrab, who kept up a constant hullabaloo of taunts, were the whole audience. "Give him the ole one-two, Arthur!" he yelled. "Aw, you ham, Arthur!" "Uppercut him, Tyma!" "Aw, you're rotten, Tyma! He was wide open then. He left a space as big as a barn door." "Aw, you're just a pair of sluggers!" he was calling one moment in assumed deep bass notes. "Sister, don't hit brother!" he was calling the next moment, in a high contemptuous falsetto. Then it became evident that Scrab, for some reason, wanted to see Tyma win. "Left hook! Tyma!" he screamed. "Straight to the jaw, Tyma!" "On the button! Tyma!"

Scrab's yells had a sudden, definite and terrifying effect. It was obvious that what he had boasted was true. He knew the fight game. And, in addition, there was something horribly compelling about his cries. Arthur and Tyma began to fight as they had never fought before, in deadly earnest.

"Soak him, Tyma!" The yells increased in fury. "Kill him, Tyma!" "There you go, boy!" "You'll have him on the ropes in another moment!" "Aw, you sissy!" "Give him a poke! Tyma!" "On the beezer, Tyma!"

Suddenly Tyma obeyed Scrab's injunction. He hit

Arthur in the face. Arthur backed, slipped, fell. The blood began to pour from his nose. Scrab burst into shrieks of laughter. "Get into your corner, Tyma!" "It'll be a K.O. before long. Look at the claret!"

"Arthur," Tyma faltered, "I'm sorry! I—I—"

But Arthur paid no attention either to the apologizing Tyma or to the yelling Scrab. At the back of the gym was a little bathroom. Arthur retreated to it, followed by Dicky and Harold. Arthur turned the cold water on in the washbowl, wet a cloth, held it for a long moment to his nose. Not one of the boys said a word. Presently the bleeding stopped.

In a few moments, Arthur strode out of the bathroom. Scrab had kept up his jeering comment, but Tyma had said nothing. "Take off the gloves, Tyma," Arthur ordered, "and come down in the Bosky Dingle with me."

"I'll come too," Scrab announced hilariously. "I'll referee the match."

Arthur turned to Harold and Dicky. "Don't wheel him out of this gym until we come back," he ordered.

"We'll keep him here, Arthur," Harold agreed.

The two boys, Arthur leading, crossed the road. No one outside the gym took note of their progress. The grownups were all indoors, the girls, working in the garden at the back of the house. Arthur strode down the steep path of the Bosky Dingle. Tyma followed. Suddenly Tyma struck a slippery place. He slid, slipped, fell forward against Arthur. Arthur went down, and Tyma going down, rolled after him and set Arthur into motion again. The two boys arrived in a tangled heap at the bottom of the Bosky Dingle, Arthur's foot resting comfortably on Tyma's face.

They scrambled to a sitting position and glared at each other. Suddenly Arthur burst out laughing. Tyma exploded too. For a few moments they continued to sit on the ground, screaming with mirth.

"To think that we let that—that—that—" Arthur appeared to be hunting for a word sufficiently disgraceful to fit Scrab. But he gave up the search. "—make trouble between us!" he ended.

"If we were to tell Robin Hood this," Tyma said, "he'd send him back to that Home he came from."

Arthur shook his head. "We won't tell on him," he declared.

"No," Tyma agreed, "we won't!"

"We brought him down here to cure him," Arthur asserted, "and, by jiminy, we're going to cure him!"

"Yes," Tyma agreed. "But we won't let him make any trouble between us again."

"Shake, Tyma!" Arthur suggested.

Still sitting on the ground, the two boys shook hands. Presently they arose and returned to the gym.

"How about it, youse guys?" Scrab called derisively as they entered. "Tyma the Mauler and Arthur the Slugger! Did you do a good job beating each other up?"

"Beating each other up!" Arthur repeated. "Why, what do you mean, Scrab?"

"Beating each other up!" Tyma repeated. "Why, Arthur and I just went for a little walk through the Bosky Dingle!"

Scrab stared at them hard. But there was no mark of fighting on either of them. "Going to try it again?" he demanded.

"Sure!" Arthur answered.

The two boys put on the gloves again. Scrab tried his hardest to work them both up to a fighting rage. But it was as though they did not hear him. They remained as cool as though they were running the lawn mower. After a while, Scrab's yells ran down, stopped. After two rounds, for which Harold again held the stop watch, Tyma and Arthur agreed they had had enough.

They undressed, took a shower and redressed, talking busily all the time and all on subjects other than boxing.

"Well, fellows," Scrab greeted them on their return, "I guess it's time for me to take my morning lay-down. Home, James!" he added with humorous intent as Arthur placed himself at the back of his chair.

Arthur wheeled Scrab to his room. But the other boys lifted him out of the chair, put him on the bed. When they returned to the little House they found Arthur in the living room, reading.

The place seemed deserted. Bunny and Robin had gone marketing. Granny, Mrs. Dore and the two babies were upstairs. From outside came the chatter of the girls as they continued to work in the garden.

Arthur looked up from his magazine. "Gee!" he said to the trio of boys.

"Gee!" they answered.

"It looks as though *Gee* was going to be our password!" Arthur commented. He added, "Let's not say anything to anybody about Scrab."

VI

Scrab and Maida and Rosie

THAT AFTERNOON the four boys accompanied Robin Hood on a purchasing expedition to Satuit. The sun had come out, warm and brilliant. They established Scrab on the lawn in his wheelchair, a table with a pile of books and magazines beside him.

For a moment, the Little House seemed to surge with activity. The beach wagon went off with the boys and with Midge and Laura, who, at the last moment decided to go with them. Mrs. Dore came downstairs, leading Delia by the hand. Delia carried an elephant and a rabbit. "Scrab, can we leave Delia here with you for an hour or so?" Mrs. Dore asked. "Granny and I would like to walk up to the Maybury farm to make a call."

"Sure!" Scrab answered.

"I don't think she'll try to run away," Granny declared.

"If she does, I'll call her back," Scrab asserted.

"I guess she'll come," Granny said, but she said it a little doubtfully.

"If I call her, she'll come," Scrab announced.

In the doorway Mrs. Dore called up the stairs, "Silva, will you stay in, please, until we get back? I am afraid Nesta may be coming down with a cold. It's so windy I don't want her to go out."

"All right!" Silva answered. "I won't leave her."

Talking busily, the two ladies disappeared up the road.

"Sab! Sab!" Delia said, running to the wheelchair. "Take up!" she commanded, lifting her arms high.

Scrab lifted her, held her in his lap for a few moments. He whispered in Delia's ear and the little girl laughed as though this were a beautiful new game. Scrab's hard eyes turned soft.

From upstairs, he caught Rosie's voice. "I'm going down to the Magic Mirror and read," she declared. "Will you lend me some of your short books, Maida?"

"Of course," came Maida's voice.

"I'll bring my basket into your room," Rosie explained. "And you choose for me!"

"All right!" Maida agreed.

Swiftly but gently, Scrab lifted Delia off his lap, placed her on the ground. "Now play with your toys, Delia," he commanded.

Obediently Delia pattered over the grass to where her toys lay, and began to play with them.

Rosie, carrying a basket, in which lay Maida's books, appeared next. She stopped at Scrab's chair.

"We're both readers this afternoon," she remarked. "Oh, there are some wonderful pictures in that *Geographic*," she informed him, "of Yellowstone Park, most of them in color, with lots of bears. Wait, I'll find them for you."

She placed her basket on the table, picked up the magazine and hastily riffled its pages. Her back was turned to Scrab. His glance fell on the basket. Suddenly his eyes turned as hard as iron. Swiftly but noiselessly, his hand went out, seized the top book, placed it under him.

"Here it is!" Rosie said. "Oh, you'll like those pictures!" Humming, she seized her basket and disappeared in the direction of the Bosky Dingle.

Scarcely had she disappeared when Scrab, first looking in every direction, withdrew the book from under him. He wheeled his chair close to the road and threw the book over it as far as he could pitch it. It fell in the high grass across the way and sank out of sight. Scrab wheeled himself back to the table.

Silence fell on the Little House. Scrab examined the pictures in the magazine, but apparently he was thinking of something else. A sneering smile kept appearing on his lips.

After a while, Granny Flynn and Mrs. Dore reappeared. They thanked Scrab for his care of Delia. "Say good-bye to Scrab, baby!" Mrs. Dore ordered. The little girl kissed and hugged Scrab. Mrs. Dore scooped the child up into her arms. Granny Flynn gathered up the toys. They disappeared. Zeke appeared with a good-natured grin and a "Time for your nap, Scrab," wheeled Scrab into his room and lifted him onto the bed.

But Scrab did not sleep. He tossed and turned from side to side as though something troubled him.

Another hour drifted by and soon the Little House exploded with voices, laughter, activity. Bunny, Robin, the two girls and the four boys had returned with the back of the beach wagon filled with bundles. Silva came down from upstairs, leading Delia. Rosie, carrying her basket, appeared at the head of the path coming up from the Bosky Dingle. The Big Eight scattered to various pursuits until only Maida and Rosie and Delia were left on the lawn. The two girls sat down. Delia busied herself at their feet with a Teddy bear and an elephant.

"How did you enjoy *At the Back of the North Wind*, Rosie?" Maida asked.

"*At the Back of the North Wind*"? Rosie repeated. "You didn't put that in the basket."

"Oh yes," Maida said, "I put it on top. It's my favorite book, and you know how hard I've tried to make you read it."

"Maida," Rosie said, "I just hate to contradict you, but that book was *not* in the basket."

"Rosie," Maida returned in a firm voice, "as sure as I'm sitting here, I put that book on top of the pile!"

"But it wasn't in the basket, I tell you, Maida," Rosie declared.

"But it *was*, Rosie. I put it there, I tell you."

Rosie's eyes flashed. Her cheeks were always a

warm scarlet, but now her whole face became red—an unpleasant brickish red. "Maida!" she exclaimed, "are you accusing me of telling you a lie?"

Maida's face had not flushed, but her eyes had become darker, and her lips had set themselves in a firm line. "I'm not accusing you of anything, Rosie," she said steadily. "I'm only saying that I'm sure I put that book on top of three others. The others were slim books, *The King of the Golden River*, *The Story of a Short Life* and *Black Beauty*. *At the Back of the North Wind* was on top. I wanted you to read it first."

Rose picked up her basket from the lawn. She lifted the books in it, "There are only three here, Maida. You can see for yourself."

"There *were* four," Maida asserted.

The two girls looked each other straight in the eyes, and for a moment, friendliness had vanished from their faces.

Then Delia spoke. "Sab frow book," she said. "Sab frow book!"

Maida and Rosie stared at Delia and then at each other.

"Where did Sab throw the book, Delia darling?" Maida asked.

But Delia was no longer interested. She placed the rabbit on the elephant's back and when it fell off, she crowed with delight.

"He couldn't leave his chair," Maida said, "so he couldn't have thrown it far."

With one accord, the two girls arose and raced

across the road, searching the high grass. Suddenly Rosie came across *At the Back of the North Wind* spread out as it had fallen, the two open pages damp with the dew from the bushes. She wiped off the open pages with her handkerchief, closed it and held it out to Maida.

Maida took it. "We can't talk about this here, Rosie," she whispered. "Come upstairs! We must never tell anyone about it."

Their arms were around each other as they walked upstairs.

VII

Scrab and Dicky, Harold, Silva and Laura

ANYONE STUDYING the Big Eight carefully the next morning would have noted an air of tension among most of them. Only Silva and Laura were their accustomed, carefree selves.

After breakfast the Big Eight scattered to their various household chores. Arthur wheeled Scrab onto the lawn where, as always, he sat in the shade of one of the big twin wineglass elms, with a table beside him covered with books. To him after a while came Dicky. He was carrying his violin. He sat down beside Scrab.

"Want me to play for you?" he asked, his face lighting with its gay, happy smile.

"I guess I can stand it if you can," Scrab answered. "Go to it."

Dicky stood up, placed the pad on his shoulder and lifted his bow. He played the "Intermezzo" from *Cavalleria Rusticana,* and the "Volga Boat Song." He lost himself in his music, as was customary with him, and presently he was walking up and down the lawn, as unconscious of where he was as though he were floating on clouds. His eyes, fixed on his instrument, were full of dreams. At the last note, he seemed to wake up.

"I didn't mean to play so long," he said. "But once I get started I forget about everything else."

Dicky placed his violin on the table. "I was wondering, Scrab," he suggested falteringly, "if you would like me to teach you how to play the fiddle. I don't think I'd be much of a teacher and I don't know a terrible lot. But you could use Strad—"

"What do you mean—Strad?" Scrab demanded.

"Stradivarius, Dicky explained, "was a great violinmaker who lived in the Middle Ages. People who own a Stradivarius violin always call it a Strad. I just named my fiddle after him. Robin looked him up in the encyclopedia and told me all about it. Real Strads are very rare today and very expensive—they cost thousands and thousands of dollars. Guarnerius was another great violinmaker. Mr. Westabrook has a Strad over at the Big House. I've seen it many times, but I've never seen a Guarnerius. What do you say, Scrab? Would you like to begin lessons today?"

"I sure wouldn't," Scrab answered promptly and in a voice full of contempt. "What good would it do me to learn to play? I never could afford to buy a fiddle, and I don't want one anyway. A fiddle! Gee! Men ought not to play fiddles. I'd feel like a sissy."

Dicky colored so deeply that his face became almost

purple. It was not with embarrassment. It was rage. For a moment, he started to lash out at Scrab. But he remembered Arthur's words: "We brought him here to cure him and, by jiminy, we're going to cure him." He thought, with an even deeper shame, that it had been his own proposal to bring a lame boy to the Little House. Dicky clenched his hand and set his teeth. When Scrab had finished, he was able to say in a quiet voice, "I see. In that case, of course you would not want to learn to play. I'll put the violin back in the closet where I keep it."

"Wait a moment," Scrab commanded. "You've played to me. Now I'm going to play to you."

Scrab drew a harmonica from his pocket. He placed it to his lips.

Undoubtedly, Scrab was master of the harmonica —Dicky admitted that immediately. He played a medley of music—marches, popular songs, sentimental and patriotic. And gradually all the upstairs windows in the Little House filled with listeners— Mrs. Dore and Granny, the girls of the Big Eight. The boys came dashing around the corner of the house from where they had been working in the garden. As Scrab brought his concert to a close, they all applauded loudly.

"Oh, play us something else! Scrab," Silva begged.

Scrab acceded. He started "How Can I Bear to Leave You?" He played it with such deep feeling that it was as though a sob ran through the music. His eyes softened. Dreams filled them. And then suddenly it was as though some dreadful memory poured a poison of hatred into his mind. He stopped short in the middle of a chord. With a half-smothered exclamation that no one of them could make out, he threw the harmonica as far as he could hurl it.

There was an instant of shocked quiet on the part of his listeners. Then the figures disappeared from the windows. The boys went back to their gardening. Dicky went over to the spot where the harmonica had fallen, picked it up.

"I'll keep this for you, fellow," he said quietly, "until you want it again. Then you ask me for it."

"I don't want ever to see it again," Scrab said. He leaned his head back against the chair and shut his eyes. Dicky was frightened at the whiteness of his face.

"I'll wheel you into your room," Dicky said. "I guess it's time for the morning lie-down."

"I guess it is," Scrab agreed in a flat voice.

But the boys of the Big Eight had not fired their last shot.

That afternoon, when seemingly much refreshed from his morning nap, Scrab sat on the lawn, Harold approached him. Harold was carrying a book.

"I thought you might be interested, Scrab, to see my stamp collection," he suggested. Opening the book he put it on the table in front of Scrab.

"I'll look at anything once," Scrab commented indifferently.

Harold took no notice of this remark. "You see, my father works for an importer," he went on, "and they get letters from all over the world. My father's boss told him that he could have all the foreign stamps, and when I was just a little boy he began bringing them home to me. At first I wasn't much interested. But father began showing me on the map the countries they came from, and pretty soon I got awfully interested. I began to save up my spending money to get more stamps, and then I met two other boys who were collecting stamps, and we used to exchange."

He paused to open his book.

"So what?" Scrab asked insolently.

Harold paid no attention to the comment. "It was really curious what happened," he went on. "Up to the time I began to get interested, I hated geography. But the moment I began to wonder what the countries that my stamps came from were like, geography began to be—well, thrilling to me. I found on the map, myself, the countries my stamps belonged to. My father used to look those countries up in the encyclopedia and tell me about them."

"Doesn't interest me!" Scrab drawled.

Without a word, but with one long, steady look at Scrab, Harold closed his book and retired to the barn.

But Scrab had not finished for the day.

Soon after, Silva appeared on the lawn where he sat in his wheelchair.

"I'm going to do some painting this afternoon, Scrab," she said with the friendliest of smiles. "Would you mind if I worked here?"

"No," Scrab drawled. He drew the word out as

though he were a little uncertain whether he wanted Silva there or not.

"I'll bring my things out," Silva said, apparently taking no notice of Scrab's tone. She made three trips into the house, returning first with a small, light, collapsible wooden table, then with her paper pad, box of paints, a tumbler of brushes, finally with a small pitcher of water.

She set up the table, opened the box of water colors, ranged her brushes in a neat file, drew up a chair and sat down.

"Have you ever done any painting, Scrab?" she asked.

"Not so you'd notice it," Scrab remarked. "I'm no sissy."

"There's nothing sissy about painting," Silva started hotly. But she controlled herself and continued. "Most of the great painters of the world have been men, and many of them were brave men. You ought to read the life of Michelangelo."

"Think so?" Scrab rejoined. "I can get along without it."

Silva did not speak for a few moments. She was busy on the part which she found always required the greatest concentration. That was putting on the pad, in pencil, what artists call the composition—the sketch which later they cover with color.

All the time, Scrab appeared to be unconscious of what she was doing, but occasionally he cast a swift, secret look in her direction.

"There!" Silva exclaimed after a while. "You see

I've sketched out the road, the trees and bushes and the path going down to the Bosky Dingle. Now I'll work with color. That's more interesting, Scrab."

With her brush, Silva transferred a little water into the tiny, shallow white china dishes which lined one side of her paint box. She selected her brush, dipped it into the water and began transferring paint from the green and blue cakes to the little saucers. "Have you ever noticed, Scrab," she went on, "that some green trees have a good deal of blue in them?"

"Blue in green trees!" Scrab repeated. "You're crazy."

Silva laughed the soft, low peal which was one of her great charms. "I don't wonder you say I'm crazy," she said. "Bunny took me to a lecture by a painter once, and he told how some artists see blue when others see rose or see green. He showed some pictures in color which proved what he said. I think," she added thoughtfully, "I myself see blue."

"The looney-bin for you!" Scrab commented.

Silva did not speak. She bit her lips. And then, apparently thinking no more about Scrab, she devoted herself to her picture.

Scrab gave the growing scene one furtive glance, then another and another. After a while he abandoned all pretense of secrecy and watched every move Silva made.

The trees began to take shape on Silva's paper. The bushes turned from green blobs to leaves and branches. The road appeared. The path to the Bosky Dingle outlined itself.

Silva could not have been unaware of Scrab's close study of her work. She said nothing, however, until she had put in the last stroke.

"Now," she said, "bad as it is, I guess it's as good as I can make it. Perhaps I'll do better the next time."

Like all Silva's work, it was a little quivery and uncertain. And yet, there was something about it that made the observer feel that the scene was a real one —it had a sense of life.

Silva held it off and studied it, frowning. "Yes, I guess it's as good as I can make it now," she concluded and her voice was a little disappointed. She added modestly, "I'll give it to you, Scrab, if you want it."

Scrab answered promptly, "What would I do with a thing like that? I don't want it. You can put it the wastebasket for all I care."

For a moment Silva did not speak. But she arose and carried her painting implements into the house. As she started for the Little House for the last time, she stood by Scrab's side an instant, holding the folded table.

"Scrab," she said, "you seem to be trying to make us think that you're the rudest and most disagreeable boy who ever lived. I don't know how the others feel about it, for we have never talked about it. But I don't believe that of you. I believe you can be as decent as anyone else if you want to."

She turned and marched toward the house.

For a moment Scrab did not speak, but as Silva opened the door, he got the better of his own surprise. "P'raps I don' want," he said and grinned a sneering grin in her direction.

Later, after Scrab had had his afternoon lie-down, Tyma wheeled him onto the lawn again.

"Scrab, you're beginning to burn," Tyma remarked. "Does your face hurt?"

"Not at all," Scrab replied loftily.

"After a while, it will turn brown," Tyma informed him, "and then you'll have a great tan. Is there anything I can do for you, Scrab? Would you like me to wheel you up the road a piece, or would you rather talk?"

"I'd like to sit and read alone," Scrab replied, taking up a book.

"All right," Tyma agreed cheerfully. He disappeared in the direction of the barn.

Scarcely had he vanished than Laura and Midge appeared in the path opposite. Laura was dressed in a Scottish costume. She wore kilts and stockings the green and blue of the Black Watch plaid, a ruffled white blouse, a Glengarry hat and a sporran. She carried two unsheathed swords.

"We've been down to the Fairy Ring," Laura explained to Scrab. "I've been dancing for Midge. As soon as she gets well, I'm going to teach her to dance."

"What makes her think she's going to get well?" Scrab inquired.

Laura and Midge both stared hard at him.

"The doctor told her she was," Laura answered.

"And he knows," Laura paused for a tiny sarcasm, "a
—little—more than you."

Scrab changed the subject. "What's the Fairy
Ring?" he asked.

"It's a great circle in the grass," Laura explained,
"that's very green. There was a round icehouse there
once, when they used to cut ice from the pond.
Bunny thinks that the grass grew greener because it
was always wet there. I like to practice dancing in
the Fairy Ring better than anywhere else."

"It's lovely over on the other side of the road,"
Midge said. "There's a big ledge of rock, called House
Rock, where Maida used to play dolls when she was
a teeny, weeny girl. And after you go through the
Bosky Dingle you come out on a lovely pond—the
Magic Mirror, Maida calls it. The Big Eight skate
there in the winter and swim there in the summer. Oh,
I'll be so glad when you can walk through the Bosky
Dingle and see it all."

"I'll never walk again," Scrab declared.

"Scrab, you mustn't talk like that," Laura scolded
him. "Of course you're going to walk again! And
what fun it will be to take you to all those places!"

Scrab's ice-cold eyes surveyed her. He sneered.
"What are those swords you're carrying for?" he
asked.

"I've been dancing a sword dance for Midge,"
Laura replied. "Shall I dance it for you?"

"I guess I can take it if you can," Scrab responded.
"Where'd you get the swords?"

"Mr. Westabrook lent them to me."

Laura crossed the swords on the ground. Then lifting onto her toes, she glided back and forth among them. It seemed, each instant, as though she were about to cut herself on the blades, but she did not touch them once. Scrab watched her carefully. He said nothing, however, until she had finished. "Gee!" he exclaimed then, "you call that a dance? I call it just a toe-tickle."

Laura did not speak, but the color ran thick under her blonde skin until it disappeared into the mass of her brown hair. She picked up the swords. "Let's go upstairs, Midge," she said, choking.

She started towards the door.

Midge stopped at Scrab's side and looked him square in the eye. "I hate you, Scrab!" she hissed.

Scrab only grinned.

VIII

Indignation

THE NEXT DAY was fair. At breakfast, Robin Hood said, "Midge and Scrab, I'm sorry to have to tell you that today, Bunny and I will have to take you both to Boston. It's business—the signing of papers. However, as there is still a little shopping Bunny wants to do for you, it will be convenient to have you where she can consult you."

"Thank you very much," Midge replied with her natural courtesy. "Of course I don't want to leave the Little House—ever—" she admitted, "but it will be fun going into shops."

"I'd just as soon be there as here," Scrab remarked indifferently.

Neither Bunny nor Robin, as it happened, caught this remark, for at that moment, Zeke entered with a message for the Hoods. But, the Big Eight heard and, for fear they would look indignantly at each other, with one accord dropped their eyes to their plates.

Soon after breakfast, Zeke brought the beach wagon in front of the Little House. The back seats had again been removed, and Robin Hood and Zeke lifted Midge and Scrab in their wheelchairs into the beach wagon. "I don't believe I need to go in a wheelchair," Midge protested plaintively.

"I know you don't, Midge," Bunny said tenderly, "but I'm so afraid you'll get tired. Next time you shall sit on a cushion," she promised gaily, "and sew a fine seam and feed upon strawberries, sugar and cream."

"I'd sit on burning coals to please you, Bunny," Midge replied.

Standing in the door, the Big Eight waved goodbyes. Maida kept her eyes on the beach wagon until it was out of sight. Then she addressed the group.

"Big Eight," she said in what was a strange voice for Maida, it was so stern and commanding. "After you've finished your chores, I want you all to meet me at the Magic Mirror. There's something I want to talk over with you."

"All right, Maida," Arthur answered for all of them.

Never was household work done so swiftly. The girls finished first and then proceeded in a group to the pond. The boys, racing down one side of the Bosky Dingle and up the other, came in a flying Indian file.

"Let's sit down," Maida suggested. "This talk may last quite a long time!"

They seated themselves on the grass.

Climbing higher each minute, the sun was getting brighter and brighter, hotter and hotter. It played on the surface of the pond and seemed to be dropping into the smooth water avalanches of silver coins. It played among the foliage of the trees and turned the tender, green young leaves into golden coins.

"You don't have to tell us what we're going to talk about, Maida," Arthur said. "It's Scrab!"

"It *is* Scrab," Maida agreed. "I think the first thing we all ought to know—is what he's been doing to us. We girls have talked over the strange experiences we've had with him. And as it's always ladies first, I'm going to ask Rosie and Silva and Laura to tell you their stories. After that—if you're willing—we want to hear if anything's happened to you four boys. But let's tell our stories as—as—well, without any feeling of dislike, as far as Scrab is concerned—as though we were reciting a lesson in geography."

Everything went as Maida planned. Silva told the episode of her painting; Laura, of the sword dance. Then Rosie described the incident of *At the Back of the North Wind*.

The boys made no comment, although the expressions on their faces changed. Particularly the two brothers showed their wrath. Tyma scowled over Scrab's treatment of Silva, and Harold clenched his fists while he listened to Laura.

But none of them made any comment.

"Now you boys!" Maida said. "We'll listen to you alphabetically—Arthur first; then Dicky; then Harold; then Tyma."

Arthur began at once. But as Tyma's narrative was the same as his, Arthur turned to Tyma occasionally to ask him to confirm a fact or an impression. The sisters were no more indignant than their brothers had been, but they showed it more. Laura had to shut her lips hard and tight to keep from bursting into wrathful words. Silva's eyes narrowed angrily when Tyma told how he had knocked Arthur down, had hit him so hard that his nose had bled.

After they all had finished, Maida said, "My father doesn't know anything about this. I don't think that Granny Flynn, or Mrs. Dore, or Bunny, or Robin even, suspect it. And none of us would want to tell them."

"Oh, we can't be tattletales!" Silva cried in horror.

"No, we've got to handle it ourselves," Maida agreed. "But how can we? That's why I decided to have this meeting."

"We boys talked it over," Arthur put in, "and we decided that we ought to keep Scrab here. We asked for him and we're stuck with him."

"Besides," Dicky added, "the more he needs it, the more we ought to help him."

"He certainly needs it," Silva said softly. "It isn't just his body that's lame. His heart is lame."

"Oh, how wonderfully you've put it, Silva!" Maida exclaimed in admiration. "That's exactly what's the matter with Scrab. His heart is lame."

"The queer thing about it," Arthur declared thoughtfully, "is that I *could* like Scrab!"

The others agreed that they could like him too—

all except Rosie. "I just detest, hate, despise and abominate him!" she exclaimed.

"Before we go any farther," Maida declared after they had finished laughing at Rosie, "I want to tell you boys that, before you came, we girls had decided exactly as you decided. We asked to have a lame boy sent here, and we've got to keep on trying to help him until he gets so well that he'll change."

"I think the thing to do," Harold suggested, "is to pay no attention to these remarks of his, although I admit they're pretty hard to take. Don't answer him back, just act as though we didn't hear him. And keep on doing everything we can for him."

"That's going to be pretty hard for me," Rosie complained. "You know I've got a quick temper. I've tried to learn to control it, and generally I do. But Scrab! He certainly rubs me the wrong way!"

"He certainly rubs me the wrong way, too," Harold agreed. "I keep finding myself doubling my fists. Sometimes I just want to smash him in the face!"

"Harold!" his sister protested in a shocked voice. Then she laughed. "I know just how you feel. Yesterday, when he said that dreadful thing about my dancing, I nearly smacked him with one of the swords!"

The Big Eight burst into a roar of laughter at the picture of Laura hitting Scrab with the flat of a sword.

"Well," Maida concluded, "there doesn't seem to be much difference of opinion among us. We all think we've got to be as nice to Scrab as we can be, just as though he was being as nice to us as he could be. We mustn't notice anything unpleasant he says and we must do everything we can for him."

"I guess that's what we've decided," Rosie agreed, "but—goodness! How I'm going to hate to do it!"

Recognizing that in describing herself, Rosie had described all of them, the Big Eight laughed again.

"I'll be as gentle as a cooing dove," Arthur promised in a high falsetto voice.

"I shall be as kind as a dear little curly lamb," Tyma vowed in as deep a voice as he could command.

"Well, I shall roar like a lion, every time I speak to him," Rosie threatened.

"And I shall growl like a bear every time he speaks to me," Laura declared.

The prospect of this animal-like behavior so delighted the Big Eight that, until Bunny and Robin returned late that afternoon, whenever they spoke, they addressed Arthur as "Dove," Tyma as "Lamb," Rosie as "Lion" and Laura as "Bear." Arthur always responded with a sweet *coo*, Tyma with a gentle *baa*, Rosie with a roar and Laura with a growl.

Bunny and Robin returned their usual gay, understanding selves. Midge was radiant.

"I don't feel the least bit tired," she exclaimed as Robin lifted her on to the ground. "Already I feel so much better. But, oh, how glad I am to get back to the Big Eight and the Little House. Sometimes in the morning I'm afraid to open my eyes, for fear it's all a dream. And sometimes when I'm talking with you, I feel that you'll all suddenly disappear."

"I'll pinch you," Maida threatened. And did. "Are we all still here?"

"You certainly are!" Midge informed them joyously.

Rosie was the first to speak to Scrab, who looked white and exhausted. "I hope you're glad to get back, too, Scrab," she said politely.

"It doesn't make any difference to me where I am," Scrab replied, "there or here."

A black look came into Rosie's face. But before she could speak, Arthur growled loudly. In spite of her rage, Rosie laughed. The whole Big Eight laughed.

"What are you guys snickering over?" Scrab demanded.

"A private joke, Scrab," Arthur informed him.

IX

The Farm

MIDGE, all this time, was changing before the very eyes of the Big Eight into a different girl.

She kept out in the air all day long. Her face had burned, then peeled, then tanned. After weeks of good country milk, cream, butter and eggs, her face had filled out. Everything about her radiated health. Her eyes were like brown pools of liquid fire. When she passed from the shade to the sunlight, her hair seemed to turn into flame. But still she hopped from spot to spot on the level ground, used her crutch on rough roads and on slanting paths.

She wanted to engage in every activity the girls offered her. Some, of course, were beyond her strength, but she put her whole heart into anything she did. Rosie asked her if she would like to learn to cook. Midge acceded happily. Every afternoon, the two shut themselves up in the kitchen. Soon Midge had learned to make biscuits, gingerbread, cookies, baked apples and fudge. Silva asked her if she would like to learn to paint. Midge acceded rapturously. Every morning, the two little girls found a paintable spot and, each sitting at a separate table, tried to paint it. Silva knew nothing about teaching. All she could do was to paint the picture before them and—explaining each step as she went along—get Midge to copy her.

"I'm afraid I'll never make an artist," Midge commented dolefully to Maida, handing her for critical comment her latest water color.

Maida examined it carefully. "It's better than I can do," she commented. "You ought to see a study of the rocks at the lighthouse that I produced. I finally tore it up."

"I guess I'll tear this up," Midge said.

"Oh no, no!" Maida protested. "You've done so much better than I. Of course," she added honestly, "it is not so good as Silva's work. But Silva has a gift. We can't any of us expect to paint as well as she."

"I know that," Midge declared. "Well, I'll try a little longer."

All Maida could do for Midge was to help her with the lessons that Bunny taught them. Midge was far behind the rest of the girls. There seemed to be nothing she wanted more in the world than to catch up. Maida showed her how to look up words in the dictionary or articles in the encyclopedia. Maida took her—on the map—to every place that she had visited in Europe with her father. She made lists of words that Midge misspelled and listened to her respelling until she learned them. Every night, she made Midge put together a big jigsaw puzzle of the United States. Gradually, working together, the two girls became so swift at this game that they started a match to see which one could first bound every state in the Union. Midge won this contest. She was adept at figures, and as Maida was woefully behind, she drilled Maida in every lesson in arithmetic that Bunny gave them.

Scrab, in the meantime, kept as close as he could to the uneventful schedule of his days. Every morning and every afternoon, interrupted only by periods of lying down, he sat outdoors in the sun. At first, when the boys invited him to the gym, he accepted every invitation. But it soon became evident that he accompanied them only to laugh at them, to toss jeers at them, to make trouble between them. By tremendous efforts, the boys managed to ignore all this. Occasionally when Arthur, his face black with rage, was tempted to answer Scrab, a warning *"Coo!"* from Tyma would make him laugh. And when, involuntarily, Tyma clenched his fists, a soft *"Baa!"* from Arthur would bring back his grin. By helping each other, the boys managed to ignore Scrab's insults. But the atmosphere of the Little House was much less friendly than it had always been.

And discovering that he could make no trouble between the boys, Scrab refused all their invitations. He continued to sit out in the sun, to pore over magazines and to read the books of adventure with which Robin supplied him.

The situation, as far as Scrab was concerned, was

much easier for the girls than the boys. The girls did not, of course, invite him to join their special activities. But in passing him, they always stopped for a polite little chat. Quivering with indignation at first, each confided to the other three what Scrab had said to them. It was Silva who finally suggested that none of them repeat these unpleasant remarks.

"It only makes us hate—I mean dislike—Scrab more," she explained, "and it doesn't do any good."

But as the four boys were usually together when they encountered Scrab, all heard what he said.

One form of entertainment Scrab did get. That, curiously enough, was his association with Delia. Delia grew fonder and fonder of him, and although it was evident that Scrab was trying to conceal it, he grew fonder and fonder of her. For long periods she sat in his lap, babbling an unintelligible string of baby confidences to him. And even when she sat on the grass, alone with her toys, she kept up a constant conversation. Scrab could not have understood her. Indeed, no one could have gathered what Delia was trying to say. But he put in an occasional "Yes, Delia!" or "No, Delia!" and the little girl seemed quite satisfied.

In the meantime, the roguish, laughing spring had gone. Serene summer drew her golden skirts across the earth, and everywhere the land smiled with the green of growing things.

The Big Eight had long ago shed their jackets and woollen caps. Now they wore summer clothes; the boys in dungarees; the girls in simple play suits. But much of the time they spent at the Magic Mirror, swimming from one raft to the other, diving off into the water and racing to the farther shore.

With the help of the boys, Robin made what he called a palanquin. This was an armchair nailed onto a narrow platform with two carrying poles. One day Scrab got into his bathing suit. Robin lifted Scrab onto the chair and the four boys carried him to the Magic Mirror. There, he sat at the edge of the pond, dabbling his useless legs in the water, watching the activities of the swimmers and listening to their cries. What was in his mind at these moments, no one knew. His face was as blank as a sheet of paper and as hard as a rock.

"Oh," Silva wailed once to the other girls, "it breaks my heart to see him sitting so—so—silent there. Oh, I wish I could do something for him!"

"We all feel that way, Silva," Maida said earnestly, "and we've tried everything we can think of," she added sadly. "But I guess we've failed."

One day at luncheon, Bunny mentioned the May-bury farm.

"A farm!" Midge said wonderingly. "I have never seen a farm in my life."

Robin stopped eating, looked at her. But it was Scrab whom he addressed. "Scrab, have you ever been on a farm?"

"Never," Scrab answered. He added, as one suddenly remembering, "sir."

"At least," Maida thought gratefully, "he has learned one thing—to say *sir* to older men."

"We'll visit Mart's farm this afternoon," Robin promised. "And to think I never thought of that! I'm ashamed of myself. But we're so used to them here that I had forgotten what a treat a farm is to a city child."

It took two cars to carry the whole party to Mart Maybury's farm. Although Midge took her crutches wherever she went, she no longer required her wheelchair. Scrab, of course, was still confined to his chair. In their least hopeful moments, indeed, the Big Eight thought he would never leave it for good. So, as usual, Robin and Zeke took the back seat out of the beach wagon, lifted Scrab's chair into the vacant space. And though the boys had to stand on the running board, somehow with the addition of the smaller car, Bunny, Robin, Zeke and the rest of the Big Eight managed to find places.

However, no one really had time to be uncomfortable—it was so short a drive.

Mart Maybury came forward to meet them. He was a man of medium height, comfortably stout, but hard as iron. His face, perpetually tanned, was like a red-brown shellac, out of which his clear blue eyes shone with the friendliest of sparkles.

"Well, I sure am glad to see you folks," he said with a hearty cordiality that made them all feel at home at once. "And my sister Elvira'll be delighted to have a visit with you."

The Maybury house, although not large, looked very comfortable. It was clapboarded and painted white. In front was a big screened-in porch and over it grew a wisteria vine, from which in the spring hung long purple cones of blossom. In a big chair sat Miss Elvira Maybury. She half reclined and half sat up, for she was an invalid. Although there were marks of suffering on her face, Miss Elvira's expression was sweet. She was as slender as a wand, white-haired and big-eyed. She greeted all the Big Eight by name when she shook hands with them. Her eyes grew softer, if that were possible, when she greeted Scrab. And she bent over and kissed Midge.

"Mart, I've got two city children here who've never seen a farm," Robin explained.

"I'll be glad to show them this one," Mr. Maybury replied. "It's not nearly so big as some, but—well, I like it!"

"Can I take the children over to the barn?" Robin asked.

"You sure can," Mr. Maybury replied. "I'll come with you."

All around in neat rows, pushing vigorously up from the warm brown earth, the crops were growing; tiers of corn, like blades of green enamel; rows of cabbages, some a beautiful emerald, some a royal purple; lines of poles on which, in one plot, beans climbed and in another, peas; rows of lettuce, their heads a close-curled, tender green; rows of beets, their stems and leaf veins as red as rubies; onions stabbing the air with jade spikes.

But the barn, which was much bigger than the house, was as fascinating to the country-bred Big Eight as it was novel to the city children. At one side was a pigpen, so clean that Rosie said it looked as though the pigs swept and dusted it every day. In it, fast asleep, lay two fat "lady pigs," as Laura described them. They opened their tiny eyes at the hubbub the strangers created, grunted protestingly and then fell fast asleep again. Beside the barn was a big space closed in by a wire fence, in which an army of fowls—cocks, hens, chickens—scratched, fed, drank from the water runnels in their little houses, peeped, clucked, or crowed.

"I love to go into the barn," Maida said as they passed through the doors. "It's so sweet-smelling."

"So do I," agreed Silva. "And look through the door at the back. It's framing the most perfect picture for us."

And so indeed it was. The open space that the great doorway framed ran in a soft green, interrupted here and there by great trees, to the summit of a low hill. At the foot of the hill, a little brook sparkled like running, melted silver. There, cows were standing knee-deep in the cool, fresh water. At the top of the hill, the sky hung like a curtain of blue, embroidered with scattered white clouds. There, cows were standing too, as clear-cut as silhouettes, against the blue air—all, as Silva commented, pointing in the same direction.

They crowded into the barn, and immediately the odor of many seasons of stored hay wrapped them in its sweet cloud. The inside of the barn was a silvery-brown. Shadows lingered in the corners.

It was Scrab who spoke first. "Gee!" he exclaimed.

And as though that exclamation could not express all his surprise, he added, "Jiminy!"

"That's King Solomon," Mr. Maybury explained with pardonable pride. "And let me tell you I'm proud of that bull."

"I guess I'd be proud of him if I owned him," Rosie said, "but not owning him, I'm scared to death of him."

The bull stood in a corner pen, closed by a door made of wide, thick boards. He was a magnificent creature, all brawn and muscle in the body, with a fierce head held high, and flaring nostrils. His eyes grew fierce as he stared at the visitors, and he pawed the floor angrily.

"He looks," Arthur said, "as though flame ought to come from his nose when he breathes."

"He looks as though he could lick his weight in lions," Tyma commented. "Are you afraid of him, Mr. Maybury?"

"I certainly take the greatest pains not to be alone with him when he's at large," Mr. Maybury admitted.

"Do you let him go out?" Scrab asked awkwardly.

"He has his own particular pasture right beside the barn," Mr. Maybury answered. "He goes and comes through that door. You see, we can open or close it from here."

"How does he know when to come in?" Maida asked.

"His stomach tells him," Mr. Maybury said.

"There's always salt here for him to lick. That's his dessert. Or it rains, or he gets sleepy."

The bull interested all the children, but the Big Eight had seen him before. He fascinated Scrab. He wheeled his chair close to the pen and watched the powerful great creature all the time they stayed in the barn.

Presently they returned to the house. "Myra is bringing us some ginger ale and some of my Banbury tarts." Miss Elvira greeted them.

"May we help her?" Maida asked.

Miss Elvira hesitated. "Yes," she said after a moment.

The children filed through the tiny hall, past the stairway that, like the old stairway in the Little House, ran almost straight upwards, and into the big kitchen in the back. There, a rather sulky-looking girl was transferring cookies from a cooky jar to two big plates.

"We wondered if we could help bring the things outside, Myra," Maida said in her politest voice.

"I guess you can," Myra answered sullenly, without thanking them or even looking at them. "If you boys will carry the bottles and glasses, you girls can carry the plates and napkins and tarts."

In silence the children did as they were bid. Myra did not follow them to the porch. Mr. Maybury opened the bottles and poured the ice-cold ginger ale into the long glasses. The boys served the grown-ups with the drinks. The girls offered the tarts.

"What delicious tarts!" Rosie said. "I wonder if Myra would give me her recipe for them."

Miss Elvira looked embarrassed. "I made the tarts. I'll give you the recipe."

"I advise you not to ask Myra for anything," Mr. Maybury laughed. "*No* is the easiest word she says."

The party from the Little House left soon after they had drunk their ginger ale.

At home—and upstairs for a moment—Rosie said, "That Myra! I'm so sick and tired of impolite people that I don't know what to do. You know, come to think of it, I guess good manners are very important."

"They *are* important," Silva said. "They're like —" Silva paused and thought for a while. "They're like keys—magic keys—that open doors for you."

X

Mr. Westabrook and Scrab

ALL THIS TIME, the Big Eight were taking it for
granted that neither Bunny nor Robin guessed what
was going on, nor how difficult were their relations
with Scrab. In reality, both Bunny and Robin were
well aware of it. But it was their policy, as far as possible, to let the Big Eight work out their problems for
themselves. Although they had not heard all that
Scrab had said, they had heard much and guessed
more. They did not, it is true, know anything about
the fracas in the gym when Scrab worked Arthur
and Tyma up from what was a friendly boxing bout
to a real fight. Perhaps that might have alarmed
Bunny. But it is probable that, knowing boys well
and having himself once been a boy, Robin would
not have taken it very seriously. But there was discussion of the newcomers among the grownups.

All agreed that Midge was a lovable—and what
Granny called a biddable—child. As for Scrab, the

women tried, all of them, to be understanding. They did not have to try to be kind, because that they all were naturally.

"I have never seen a boy behave so badly," Bunny said thoughtfully, "but there's something about him —I like him."

"He's mean. He's contrary. He's disagreeable," Mrs. Dore declared emphatically, "but I like him."

"The poor choild!" Granny Flynn exclaimed compassionately. "With no kith nor kin in the worruld to love him, no wonder he hates everybody. He's a quare gossoon, but I like him."

"No wonder you like him, mother," Mrs. Dore smiled. "He's almost polite to you."

"It's pretty hard to be impolite to Granny," Bunny said, squeezing Granny's tiny hand. "I wouldn't even try it, for I know I'd break down and hug her."

Robin listened with interest to this conversation. "Do you know," he asked, "that you all ended what you had to say about Scrab with 'but I like him?' "

The three women looked at each other. "It's true, we did," Bunny agreed.

"What makes you like him?" Robin asked.

"I'm sure I don't know," Mrs. Dore answered frankly.

"I don't know meself," Granny declared, "but—"

"But you never disliked any child in your life, mother," Mrs. Dore teased her mother.

"I don't know why I like him either," Bunny said. So seriously was she thinking that all the dimples had left her face. Her brows were knitted and her eyes—all their merriment deepened to thoughtfulness—were gazing straight before her. "But I do like him."

"So do I, ladies," Robin said, "and, like you, I don't know why."

That night Robin called on Mr. Westabrook at the Big House and had a long talk with him.

The result of that was that three days later, the Big Eight and their two guests were invited to luncheon at the Big House.

The Big Eight loved to go to the Big House. They always felt that it was a special occasion. Perhaps, in consequence, they put an extra polish to their faces and hands. When they assembled in the Map Room of the Little House, they looked very festive. The girls wore crisp gingham dresses. But the boys, in their summer suits, their hair as smooth as satin, their faces shining from soap and water, looked, as Rosie put it, "as though they had just come out of a bandbox."

"What's this Big House?" Scrab asked, in a low voice, of Arthur. "Is it—it isn't the clink, is it?"

"It's—it's—" Arthur was beginning. "No, I won't tell you anything about it," he concluded. "I'll let you find out for yourself."

The two cars set off, the beach wagon driven by Robin, filled with Scrab in his wheelchair, Robin and Bunny on the front seat. Into the other car crowded the Big Eight and Midge, her cheeks blazing with excitement and her crutch—only one now—leaning against her knee.

It was a brief ride and a pleasant one, over the tree-bordered main road that led to the Big House. They turned into a road which swept up to the Big House, passed it and then swept back to the main road again.

"Gee!" Scrab exclaimed.

The Big House was not palatial, but it was much bigger than the Little House. It was built of white marble. On the ample lawn, which was cut to a velvet softness and smoothness, occasional great trees—elms, oaks, copper beech, purple maple—stood in pools of shadow. Across the road and beyond the lawn on both sides grew high, thick shadowy woods.

Mr. Westabrook, in white flannels, was standing on the wide terrace which ran in front of the house.

"Welcome," he called as the Big Eight tumbled out of the car and ran to greet him. "Have you noticed the weather! I had a talk with the Weather Man last night and ordered this day for you. I told him there was to be no wind and not a single cloud in the sky to get in the way of the sun."

"How kind of you, Mr. Westabrook!" Rosie commented gaily. "And I'm sure the sun is as grateful as it can be."

"Rosie," Mr. Westabrook replied, "that's just what the sun said to me when he came in my window this morning. He said, 'I'm very grateful to you, Mr. Westabrook. Today I didn't have to plow my way through clouds.' "

Scrab's face had set in its customary sneer when suddenly Mr. Westabrook advanced towards him, holding out his hand. The sneer vanished like a mist before a sudden outburst of sun. Arthur observed, with secret delight, that Scrab was frightened.

"I'm glad to welcome you here, Scrab," Mr. Westabrook greeted him cordially. "And now come, all of you, into the house. We're having luncheon on the back terrace."

Zeke wheeled Scrab through the doorway and through the wide hall which ran to the back of the house. Scrab looked hard at the two suits of armor between which his chair rolled.

They passed through the wide door onto the back terrace where stood the table. "Sit down at once!" Mr. Westabrook said. "You'll find a card with your name on it where you are to sit. Midge, being one of the guests of honor today, is to sit at my right, and Scrab, being the other guest of honor, will be at my left!"

In no time, they found their places. The cards, which were decorated with flat figures of feathered birds, were so pretty that Silva asked if she could take hers home.

"Of course!" Mr. Westabrook answered. "They're yours."

Cards disappeared into feminine handbags and into masculine pockets.

For a moment, everyone talked about the scene before them. Neither Scrab nor Midge entered into this conversation. But both looked about them. Midge's eyes grew wide with wonder. It was as though the little girl had found herself suddenly trans-

ported to fairyland. Scrab drew a curtain over his
expression. He permitted no look, either of surprise
or admiration, to come into his face.

Below the terrace spread wide flower gardens like
flung rainbows. Butterflies alighted on the satiny
petals. Robins and orioles drew streaks of dazzling
color through the air. Here and there reared a marble
bird bath or a mirrored gazing bowl. The birds, flut-
tering and twittering, congregated in the baths and
the flowers looked at their brilliant reflections in the
gazing bowls.

Beyond stretched a lawn, like that in the front of
the house, emerald green, velvet short, velvet soft. At
the foot of the lawn, two great black iron fountains
were playing. From their high, wide bowls, they sent
sheets of water upward. The sun sparkled through
the spray. The breezes blew it this way and that,
through the air. Then it fell back into the bowls.

Here, as in front, forest on both sides grew to the
edge of the lawn.

The luncheon proceeded—a simple one. First came
fruit cup made from oranges, grapefruit and peaches.
Then came roast chicken which, most expertly, Mr.
Westabrook carved, with baked potatoes and fresh
peas, beach plum jelly. Then came ice cream with
small, flat frosted cakes. All the time the butler kept
filling the children's glasses with milk.

Midge examined the table, the wonder deepening
in her eyes. The cloth was of lace. In the center lay a
huge bowl of fruit: tangerines, apples, plums, with
great bunches of grapes, purple and green, hanging

over the sides. The china was thin, exquisitely decorated. The silver was heavy and so highly polished that the sun glittered on it. The glasses looked as though they had been hollowed from crystal or ice.

The children had just finished their ice cream when Mr. Westabrook exclaimed in a whisper, "There come the deer. I was afraid they were not going to visit us today."

Beyond the fountain at the foot of the lawn, a deer family, a stag, a hind and a little fawn, emerged from the woods. They crossed the lawn slowly, browsing with mouthfuls delicately small. The little fawn stopped to drink from the fountain. The people on the terrace froze to quiet.

Scrab stared so hard that, afterwards, Robin said, "You could have knocked his eyes off his face with a ruler!"

The lovely creatures—every movement grace, every attitude a picture—disappeared into the forest on the other side of the lawn.

And then another miracle performed itself.

From under the trees what seemed to be a great bird, drawing after it a long tail, emerged. Suddenly it spread its tail upright in what was like a great round fan, embroidered in green and blue and gold. Another bird appeared from under another tree, a third and a fourth. The fourth was snowy white. All spread their tails, strutting proudly about, glistening, gleaming, glittering, in the sun, like birds made from jewelled metals.

Midge could not speak. Scrab's sneer vanished.

"What are those birds?" he gasped.

"Peacocks," Mr. Westabrook told him.

"Peacocks!" Scrab repeated.

"Peacocks!" Midge exclaimed joyfully. "At last I've seen a peacock!"

The party gazed their full at the peacocks. Presently Mr. Westabrook asked, "Is there anything inside the house that you want to show Midge and Scrab, Big Eight?"

"I'd like to show Midge the Vermeer," Silva said.

"I'd like to show her the 'littles,' " Rosie said.

"I'd like to show her the shell and the crystal," Laura said.

"I'd like to show Scrab that big Audubon book with all the colored pictures of birds in it," Tyma said.

"I'd like to show him the bronze of Julius Caesar," Arthur said.

"I'd like to show him that battle picture by Meissonier," Harold said.

"I'd like to show him—" Dicky began. But before he could finish, Scrab interrupted. "I'd like to see the Strad," he said.

"That was just what I wanted to show you!" Dicky said with a gratified smile. "So you remembered it!"

Scrab nodded carelessly.

But before they could show him anything, the doorbell rang.

XI

Scrab and Mr. Stevens and Mr. Poole

THE BIG EIGHT stood in silence. A moment later, the butler appeared on the terrace. Addressing himself to Mr. Westabrook, he announced, "Mr. Stevens and Mr. Poole, sir."

"We have callers," Mr. Westabrook commented genially. "Come in, children, and meet my guests. You'll like them both."

The Big Eight and Midge obviously liked the guests at once. Scrab's expression did not change when he looked at them.

Mr. Stevens was a giant of a man, blond, with very blue eyes that kept up a constant twinkle behind his glasses. Mr. Poole was small, thin, black-haired and black-eyed. And when he smiled, which was often, he showed an amusing dimple in one cheek.

"These young people were just about to make a tour of the house," Mr. Westabrook informed his guests. "How would you like to go with them?"

"Nothing I'd like better," Mr. Stevens answered in a gay, booming voice.

"I've always wanted to go through this place," Mr. Poole asserted, "and look as long as I liked at the things that interested me."

The two men placed themselves at the end of the procession where Arthur stood, one hand on the handle of Scrab's chair, ready to wheel him.

"Now let me see," Mr. Westabrook said, "we'll have to take things in order. We come first to the shell and the crystal at the side door."

The crowd trooped around to the side door. Arthur brought up the rear with his crippled charge, Mr. Stevens on one side, Mr. Poole on the other.

The rest of the Big Eight formed a semicircle in front of the side entrance, leaving space for Scrab's chair. Scrab faced the open halves of a door of carved wood. But he did not look at that. In front and to one side, was a huge tropical shell. It lay with its lip on the floor, as full of curves as a flower. It was as delicate a pink as a newly opened rose. On the other side, perhaps two feet high, was an enormous quartz crystal of blue—a shimmering turquoise blue which offered a perfect contrast to the shining rose pink of the shell.

Scrab stared at the two beautiful objects. He made a shuffling movement in his chair.

"We'll help you to get nearer, son," Mr. Stevens said good-naturedly. "Give us a hand, Poole!"

The two men lifted Scrab out of his chair and carried him near enough to the shell and the crystal so that he could lean down and study them.

Scrab laid his hand first on the warm satin surface of the shell and then on the cool, glassy surface of the crystal. "Gee," he exclaimed, "I didn't know there were such things! Are there many shells like that in the ocean?"

"Thousands of them, Scrab!" Mr. Westabrook informed him. "Tropical beaches are covered with shells, some as small as the head of a pin, some larger than this. This is an unusually fine specimen, of course, as far as color goes."

They proceeded next to the library, where was one of the things that the Big Eight wanted to show Midge and Scrab—the bronze Julius Caesar.

Julius Caesar stood on a malachite table. Without waiting, Mr. Westabrook's two grownup guests lifted Scrab out of his chair and again held him upright on the floor. He looked long and intently at the bronze, while Mr. Westabrook told him briefly the history of Caesar, ending with the statement that, here, he was commanding a battle in Gaul.

A strong, spirited figure, Julius Caesar stood, his hand protecting his eyes from the sun, keenly studying an enemy position. He wore the magnificent Roman armor, the majestic helmet.

"Come round behind, Scrab," Arthur called. "The armor is just as swell in the back as in the front."

Scrab made a motion in Arthur's direction, and the two guests helped him as before.

When they entered the front room, the huge book of birds, compiled by Audubon, lay flat on the great central library table. The Big Eight always looked it through when they came to the Big House. Today, however, they seemed to enjoy it even more than ever because of Scrab's interest. It took two to turn the leaves. Tyma, on one side, lifted the big page, handed it to Harold on the other side. Harold put it carefully down.

In every picture was a bird or a group of birds, flying, or settled on their nests in bushes, or in the branches of trees. Scrab looked at them as though he were staring through a peephole into a new world. He said nothing. It was obvious to all the lookers-on that he kept silence only because he had no words with which to express his feelings.

Next came the Vermeer in one of the two front rooms. Here, Silva became guide and lecturer, pointing out the beauties of this great work of a great master. Scrab made no comment. He looked hard at the picture though, and he listened to all Silva said. In the Vermeer, two Dutch women sat sewing in a room of a Dutch house. Silva pointed out the lovely flesh tints in the women's faces, arms and hands, the beautiful shadowy atmosphere of the room, the views through the open windows, the pictures that covered the walls, the tiled floor. Midge listened with a breathless interest to Silva's words, stared with a breathless intensity at the picture itself.

In the front room across the way was a battle picture of the French painter, Meissonier, which was Harold's favorite.

Here again Scrab's interest flared. He stood up in his wheelchair, and the two men lifted him to the picture so that he could examine it closely. It was tiny. Scrab had to go close to get the details. A group of French soldiers in red and blue uniforms were charging a street from the doorway of a church. Clouds of battle smoke drifted in the air. On the steps, face down, his uniform blood-soaked, lay a dead soldier.

It did not seem as though Scrab could look long enough at the Meissonier, but he made no comment.

Then came the "littles" in a cabinet in that room. The "littles" were a collection of tiny objects that Maida had gathered. There were miniature chairs and tables of Dutch silver; tiny Japanese and Chinese houses; small boxes in metal, china and wood; minnikin vases, coffeepots and teapots. These, of course, entertained everyone, but perhaps the girls more than the boys.

Last of all, Mr. Westabrook opened a door in the hall. And there, on a shelf, resting on a velvet cushion, lay a violin. Above it, an electric light burned.

"The light is to keep the violin dry," Mr. Westabrook explained. "Now I am going to pass it about, so you can all say you have held a Strad in your arms."

Mr. Westabrook took the graceful instrument, glistening brown like a chestnut, from the closet and handed it to Scrab first—"Because he asked for it!" Mr. Westabrook commented. Then he handed it to Midge and from her, to the Big Eight. It might have been a bubble, so carefully did the Big Eight hold it, so lightly did they stroke its polished surface. Dicky held it for an instant under his chin, as though he were longing to play it—which he was.

They stayed so long into the afternoon that Mr. Westabrook served tea. But the younger members of the party drank ginger ale.

Scrab whispered to Arthur that he would like to see the shell, the crystal, the Julius Caesar and the battle picture again before he left, and Arthur obligingly wheeled him close to all these treasures.

Then the party from the Little House started home.

Inside the Big House, the instant the beach wagon had departed, Mr. Westabrook asked Mr. Poole and Mr. Stevens a question. "What do you think?" he asked the one, and "Can he ever walk?" he asked the other. But this time he called them Dr. Stevens and Dr. Poole.

XII

Scrab and the Household

THAT NIGHT there was joy and jubilation, triumph and assurance, in the Little House. The four boys, walking to the Magic Mirror after supper, were full of it.

"Scrab's become a different fellow!" Harold declared, the instant they were out of hearing. "How interested he was in everything in the Big House! And he wasn't rude to anyone. Did you notice?"

"Did I notice!" Dicky repeated. "I was so surprised you could have knocked me down with a—with a—"

"Telegraph pole," Arthur substituted for the "feather" that, obviously, Dicky was searching for among the words in his vocabulary.

Dicky laughed. "All I could think of was *needle*. Anyway I could scarcely speak."

"Mr. Westabrook isn't the kind of man you'd dare to be rude to," Arthur remarked. "And those two callers, Mr. Stevens and Mr. Poole. I don't think many boys would dare to be rude to them either."

"That's true," Dicky agreed. "But I don't think Scrab felt like being rude. He was really interested in all the things we showed him."

"He certainly was interested," Tyma agreed. "And the deer and the peacocks thrilled him."

That was when Arthur said, "His eyes popped out so far you could knock them out of his head with a ruler."

"I'm sure we'll find him a different boy tomorrow," Harold declared. "And will I be glad? I'm so tired of looking into a face like a block of ice!"

"And that sneer!" Dicky added. "How many times have I felt like knocking it off his face!"

This expression of ferocity was so unlike the gentle Dicky that his companions burst into laughter. Dicky joined them rather sheepishly after a while.

"I hope the change begins tomorrow," Tyma said. "I hope we find him all merry sunshine when we wake up."

"I'm likely to burst into tears if we do," Arthur growled.

The boys laughed again. But for the rest of their walk, they talked about other things.

The girls showed their jubilation too, but only to each other. It was, however, more warm and assured than that of the boys.

Maida began it. "I was proud of Scrab today at the Big House," she burst out, as though she could not contain herself any longer, the moment they were alone. "He was so polite to everybody."

"Did you notice he's learned to say *sir* to older

men?" Laura took it up. "Oh, I was so afraid he'd be rude to Mr. Westabrook."

"If he'd been rude to Mr. Westabrook," Rosie interrupted with flashing eyes, "I'd—I don't know what I would have done! But it would have been something *dreadful*."

The other three girls laughed at Rosie's rage. And after a while, Rosie herself had to smile. "Probably I wouldn't have done anything," she admitted.

"I think Mr. Westabrook would have known how to take care of him," Silva said with a sarcastic inflection, "if Scrab had been rude to him."

"My father always knows what to say and do," Maida declared proudly. "But here we are talking about what Scrab might have done when I'm dying to talk of what he did do. I was so happy!"

"He *was* interested in all the treasures we showed him," Laura admitted.

"He was so interested," Rosie put in, "that all that hard, cold sneering look disappeared from his face. Why, he looked like a different boy!"

"Scrab has grown very handsome," Silva said. "Have any of you girls noticed it?"

"I have," declared Maida. "It surprised me, but it delighted me."

"I have," declared Laura, "but I never thought to speak of it."

"I have," agreed Rosie, "but it didn't make me like him any better."

"His face has filled out," Silva went on. She spoke slowly and her eyes caught on a point in mid-air, as though she were describing a picture she saw there. "He's got awfully tanned, sitting so much in the sun, and the brown color makes his eyes a more striking green. And his hair is just like a cap carved out of brass."

Maida sighed. "We've had a strange season at the Little House," she commented. "Not that I'm sorry we asked my father if we could stay home this summer. But sometimes I feel as though—as though trouble were hanging over us. But after this, I think it's going to be different."

"I think so too," Silva agreed.

"I feel certain of it," Laura declared.

"I *hope* so," Rosie stated.

Bunny and Robin discussed the situation too, sitting in their living room in the New Ell.

"I was quite proud of Scrab today," Bunny said. "He really behaved very well at the Big House."

"It's amazing what he's picked up just by using his eyes," Robin remarked. "He never asks any questions. But you must have noticed, Bunny, how he studies everybody."

"Indeed I have," Bunny declared. "His mother must have been a nice person. His table manners have always been good. It's mainly words or expressions he uses which make him seem so tough. He's learned to say *good morning* to all of us, and *sir* to you, and not to sit down before older people do. But there's something back of it all that I cannot understand. It's as though he hated everybody."

"There *must* be something back of it," Robin agreed. "But what it is I cannot guess. Perhaps those two doctors Mr. Westabrook had over this afternoon can give us the answer."

"I don't believe it's as serious as that," Bunny declared hopefully. "He was so nice today that I think you will find him quite a different boy tomorrow."

"I wonder," Robin said.

But Scrab was far from a different boy the next morning. Robin always helped him to bathe and dress, always wheeled him into the dining room. Scrab was sitting at his place at the table when the Big Eight, the girls coming downstairs, the boys hurrying from the barn, appeared. One look at Scrab, and all knew what they had to expect.

Scrab's face was leaden, as though he had not slept a wink. His mouth was set in two lines as straight as though drawn by a ruler. His eyes had frozen again. He replied to the greetings with a short, abrupt "Morning!" and he looked at none of them when he spoke.

After breakfast, Robin said, "Big Eight, what are you going to do after you've finished the chores?"

"Swimming!" the boys said as with one voice.

"It's a perfect day for swimming," the girls added.

"Would you like me to wheel you down to the Magic Mirror, Scrab?" Robin asked.

"No," Scrab answered decidedly. He added, after a pause, "Thank you!" He added, after another pause, "Sir."

"I'll find you some books then," Robin offered cheerfully.

"And if we put the children out," Granny Flynn asked, "will you keep an eye on them? Sure and they moind you foine."

"Yes, Granny Flynn," Scrab answered, but he did not look in Granny's direction when he addressed her.

That was the beginning of the most uncomfortable week that the Big Eight had ever passed.

Immediately on their arrival at the Magic Mirror, they held an indignation meeting. And although the girls had not again discussed the problem of Scrab with the boys, they talked as though, together, they had many times considered it and, together, come to the same conclusion.

"I'm so disappointed," Maida said. Her whole figure drooped.

"Don't tell me that boy's *ever* going to be any nicer," Rosie said with flaming cheeks and blazing eyes. "He isn't ever going to be any better. He's the horridest person I ever met in my life."

"How can he keep on the way he is?" Harold exclaimed. "How can he?"

"I don't understand, Harold," Laura answered this. "And I don't care any more. He can go his way and we'll go ours. And if we don't take any notice of him, it won't make any difference if he's halfway decent or not."

"We've done everything we could," Maida declared sadly, "and yet he hasn't noticed it. Or if he has, he doesn't care."

"He hates us," Tyma said. "And *why*, I don't know."

"First of all," Silva said, "I'm sorry for Scrab. But next I'm sorry for us because we've failed."

"Yes, we've failed," Maida agreed, still drooping. Then suddenly she straightened up. "But only for a while," she announced with determination. "We've taken on this job and we've got to do it."

"That's the way I feel about it," Dicky declared earnestly. "It was Maida and I who first spoke of getting two lame children here. When they came and we all thought it was going to turn out so well, I never said what I'm going to say. But I say it now. I am to blame. It was I who first thought of it."

"Don't talk as though you were sorry and apologizing," Maida entreated. "I thought it was the loveliest idea. And I was so mad that I didn't think of it first. I was proud of you then, Dicky. And I'm proud of you now."

"And we must remember that half of our experiment is a great success," Silva pointed out. "Look at Midge!"

Very rarely did the boys of the Big Eight praise the girls. Rarely did they even comment on them. Arthur spoke. "Midge is a swell girl!" he said.

"She certainly is," Rosie agreed. "I can't bear to think that one day she's going to leave us."

As though emboldened by Arthur's courage, the other boys added a leaf to Midge's laurels. "She's plucky. She always wants to do whatever we're doing," Harold declared.

"If she's ever in pain," Dicky added, "and sometimes I think she is—was, I mean—she never said a word about it."

"She's got plenty of nerve, too," Tyma remarked. "I know she was frightened when she first went in swimming with us. But she never peeped a peep."

"Oh, that's why you always swam beside her, Tyma!" Rosie exclaimed. "You were afraid she might get frightened and sink."

If Tyma had been caught beating Midge, he could not have blushed deeper or looked more abashed. The rest of the Big Eight laughed at him and after a moment he joined them.

"I guess there's nothing else we can do," Maida concluded, drawing a deep sigh, "but to keep on trying to help Scrab."

"I shan't try to help him," Rosie declared, turning fiery again. "I shall never do another thing for him."

However, when the Big Eight—all dried off after lying on the sandy edge of the Magic Mirror—filed across the lawn past Scrab, Rosie said, "Scrab, is there anything I can get for you?" That was characteristic of Rosie.

It was equally characteristic of Scrab that, hunched over a magazine, he answered, without even looking at her, "Naw! Beat it!"

The rest said nothing. The boys did not even look at Scrab. But their faces grew as impassive as those of a quartet of Indian braves.

A week went by. Scrab was himself exaggerated in

every way. He spoke to no one beyond "goo' morning!" and "goo' night!" and to answer questions that were put directly to him. He did not bother to thank the boys who, twice a day, wheeled him on the road in one direction or the other. Even Robin in his pleasant morning conversation could get nothing from him but a "yes, sir," or a "no, sir." It was hard to resist Bunny when she talked with him, and he seemed at least to listen to what she said. To Granny Flynn, too, he was almost polite. But Granny was busy all the time and rarely sat out on the lawn where, for longer and longer periods, Scrab seemed to live.

But Scrab never objected to taking care of the little girls. Nesta and Delia played about his chair, Delia talking to him all the time, paying no attention when he did not answer, and quite frequently coming to his side and holding her arms high as a signal to be taken up. Scrab always took her up.

One night, in the privacy of their own living room, Robin said to his wife, "Bunny, I'm completely stumped. I can't make head nor tail of that boy."

"I'm a little disheartened myself," Bunny admitted. "It's spoiling the summer for the Big Eight. But I'm proud of them. They've been such good sports."

"Yes, they have. But it's evident that they're at the end of their string as far as Scrab is concerned. I hate to admit that we've failed. I hate to send the boy back to that institution we took him from. But he's like the one bad apple in the barrel that ruins all the rest. We can't have the entire summer spoiled for the others."

"What do you think we ought to do, Robin?" Bunny asked.

"I may have to go to Mr. Westabrook and tell him we've failed," Robin replied. "How I hate to do that! Well, I'll wait two or three days."

"Wait a week," Bunny begged. "Do, Robin."

"We'll wait as long as you say, Bunny," Robin promised.

"It will break Maida's heart," Bunny declared, "to have the experiment fail."

"I know it! I know it!" Robin acknowledged. "That's what's holding me up!"

Spectacles Island

ONE MORNING, a few weeks later, the Big Eight had assembled at the breakfast table.

"Where's Dicky?" Arthur asked. And simultaneously, "Where's Midge?" Maida inquired.

"Dicky couldn't find his other sneaker," Arthur explained, with enjoyment. "He's always losing it. Where was it this time?" he inquired of the breathless Dicky who arrived, panting apologies.

"Behind the door," Dicky grinned as he made this confession. "But that was easy. Once I found it behind a picture."

"Behind a picture!" Rosie repeated in a scandalized tone. "Dicky Dore, you never did!"

"I did so," Dicky declared. "I threw it over my head and that's where it landed. I've never thrown a sneaker since," he added hastily.

"But where can Midge be?" Maida asked again.

"Oh, I hear her coming now," Bunny remarked. "Here she is! Look at her!"

The Big Eight pivoted in their chairs.

Without crutch or support of any kind, Midge was walking jauntily into the room.

"Midge!" the girls screamed.

"Good for you, Midge!" exclaimed Arthur.

"Where's your crutch?" Dicky asked.

"I can't believe my eyes!" Harold declared.

"Midge, you're *walking!*" Dicky gasped.

Scrab alone said nothing.

"This is the nicest kind of surprise, Midge," Robin complimented her. "How on earth did you manage it all by yourself?"

"I didn't do it all by myself," Midge confessed. "I did, though, in the beginning. I began practicing walking whenever I was alone—especially at night, after you girls had fallen asleep. At first I tried walking from my bed to the chair where my clothes were. That was only a few steps. And then after a while, I tried walking to the bureau and then to the door."

"What dumb bunnies we were!" Rosie said disgustedly, "not to suspect it."

"Once I walked out into the hall," Midge went on. "But then I got a little frightened of the stairs, so I told Bunny, and I asked her if she would keep it a secret until I could walk. For the last three days I could have gone anywhere, but I wanted to make sure. Oh, what a wonderful time I've had! When you were off in the car, Bunny would let me practice in her room or down by the Magic Mirror. Was I proud the first time I walked to the pond without my crutch and without taking Bunny's arm! It's been such fun for me, Bunny."

"It was fun for me too, Midge," Bunny answered. "I never shall forget the first time I saw you walk alone."

All the girls of the Big Eight got up from their seats, walked around the table to Midge and kissed her. All the boys followed and shook hands with her.

As before, Scrab said nothing.

"We're going to celebrate this day," Bunny announced. "I've planned it all out. We're going to do something you'll all love. We're going to Spectacles Island for a picnic."

"Gee!" Arthur exclaimed. "Spectacles Island! Old Spec!"

Scrab spoke for the first time. "What is Spectacles Island?" he asked.

Rosie looked at him pityingly. "Oh, Scrab, we've never happened to mention it. And as we couldn't take you up in the Tree Room to see it, we never even thought of it. It's an island in Massachusetts Bay, just off our coast. It belongs to Mr. Westabrook."

"It's shaped like a pair of spectacles," Arthur explained. "There are two round islands, with a neck of land connecting them. That neck is so narrow that from a distance Spectacles looks like two islands. The glasses of the spectacles are called Northern Eye and Southern Eye."

"We go there on picnics every summer," Laura added. "Oh, it's such a beautiful island, especially in the fall. All the colors of the bayberry and the beach plum!"

"Once we spent a long week end on Spectacles," Harold went on. "There's a house made of stone there with two big rooms. They use it for duck hunting. We call it the Stone House. We were marooned there once in a hurricane, and Mr. Westabrook had to send us provisions by airplane."

"And there's a circle of great rocks in front of the cabin, and Maida named it Stonehenge," Silva contributed.

"What's Stonehenge?" Scrab asked.

"It's a double circle of prehistoric rocks in England," Maida answered. "My father took me to visit it once."

"There are two ponds on Spectacles," Tyma broke in, "one on Southern Eye and one on Northern Eye. And what tides we have there! What combers! We'll show you the Spout."

"And once, Arthur discovered a great—" Dicky was beginning.

"Oh, was that an adventure!" Rosie sparkled.

"I never was so frightened in my life," Laura announced.

"What a terrible head he had!" Silva shuddered. "I guess I mean *terrifying*."

"You'd have thought so if you'd been me," Harold said grimly. "My head was nearest his when we carried him."

"Arthur," Maida said, "I should have thought when

you first saw him, you would have fainted dead away."

The Big Eight stopped to laugh at the picture of the stalwart Arthur "fainting dead away."

"I was frightened," Arthur admitted. "Still, I never had such a good time in my life. But he certainly was a horror!"

"What are you all chewing the rag about?" Scrab asked, his curiosity breaking through his sullenness.

"I'll tell you on Spectacles when I can point out where I saw him," Arthur decided, "and I'll tell you just what we did afterwards."

"What are we waiting for?" Tyma demanded.

Midge and the Big Eight arose as one body. They flew to their household tasks. Presently the beach wagon appeared in front of the house. Robin and Zeke lifted Scrab, chair and all, into it. The Big Eight distributed themselves about the monster hampers of luncheon in both cars, and they started off.

They proceeded in the opposite direction from the Big House. Scrab had been on that road before—as far as Arthur's vigorous muscles could wheel him. But they soon came to country that was unfamiliar to him. It was a typical country road, tree-bordered and bushy, with great, gray-ledged pastures running up or downhill on both sides. Scrab stared at it all, as though he were looking through a book illustrated with beautiful paintings.

Presently they turned a corner and there, stretching before them, in the serene, blue quiet of a windless day, lay Massachusetts Bay. And on it, floating between sea and sky like a vision—

The Big Eight greeted this dazzling picture with shouts of joy.

"Is that Spectacles Island?" Scrab asked.

"Yes!" the Big Eight all informed him in a deafening shout.

"I can see that it looks like one island," Scrab remarked.

At the foot of the road was a pier, and beside it lay a launch. On it, in brilliant letters, was painted *The Golden Hind*.

When the cars came to a stop, the Big Eight, Midge as vigorous as any one of them, stormed onto the pier. Robin and Zeke lifted Scrab's chair out of the beach wagon and onto the launch.

"Good morning, Fred," Robin greeted the young, sunburned, tow-haired captain. But the Big Eight swarmed to shake hands with him. Somehow Robin managed to insert an arm into this seething mass and to grasp the captain's hand. The luncheon was stowed away. The whole party hurried aboard and in no time, they were chug-chugging smoothly over the blue satin of the water, embroidering it in their wake with ruffles of white foam.

The water splashed and hissed. The sun poured light on them as thick and golden as honey. Gulls, as frail as paper, yet as solid as though they were cut from silver, swooped, soared and curved between sea and sky.

"Isn't this swell!" Tyma demanded.

And everyone except Scrab shouted, "Swell!"

It did not of course take long, at their rate of speed, to get to Spectacles. There, another pier, a little ramshackle and broken, protruded from the shore. Zeke and Robin lifted Scrab onto it. The Big Eight and Midge raced over it.

"I'll be back for you about five," the captain called jovially. Then the launch scuttled off. Joining the pier was a fairly good road. "Can I wheel Scrab for you, Robin?" Arthur asked.

"No, thank you, Arthur," Robin replied. "You children flock on ahead. Zeke and I will spell each other."

Midge and the Big Eight started off at a run. "If you come upon a lion or a tiger," Robin called after them, "climb a tree!"

"I hope we do!" Arthur called back.

But they ran into nothing more dangerous than a woodchuck, whose squat brown figure Tyma's sure eyes picked up across the meadow beside the road.

But birds abounded—robins, orioles, grackles, starlings, cowbirds, catbirds. Tyma even spied a hawk wheeling in the high heaven.

Presently they came to where the road opened onto a wide circle of grassy land, defined by high pines. Great round boulders and slim slabs of rock formed a big circle, so carefully placed by nature that it looked as though man had planned it.

"Stonehenge!" Maida called joyfully.

In the center of the clearing—"The Stone House!" Maida called—again joyfully.

The Stone House consisted of two rooms; one big, made of stone, a small lean-to, made of wood.

The Big Eight broke and ran to the Stone House. But once they reached it, they did not go in. They sat on the grass and waited for the others. For some time, they could hear Bunny and Robin pointing out the beauties of the way to Scrab; here, an oriole's nest; there, a little grove of white birch; yonder, an unusually big mass of puddingstone. But not once did they hear Scrab's voice.

"Isn't that Scrab the—the—" Rosie began with vigor. She ended feebly with, "the limit!"

"First of all," Robin said, as he wheeled Scrab to the edge of the porch, "let's take the walk around Southern Eye. Then we'll come back here and have luncheon. Then we'll explore Northern Eye."

"Great!" approved Arthur. And off they started.

The walk about Southern Eye was charming and interesting but uneven. The road followed the shore. The tide was coming in, although as yet, it was far from full. They saw waves that threw crests of foam upward. They saw clouds that, although so white and shining and ethereal, looked as though they might at any moment, fall upon them. They walked about the pond on the Southern Eye, the girls gathering flowers, the boys, of course, constantly straying from the path. And all of them following with their eyes the flight of the birds Robin pointed out to them.

Turning, twisting, rambling off the road and returning to it, going back and running forward, everyone calling everyone else's attention to something, it was quite two hours before they found themselves at Stonehenge again.

"Am I hungry!" Rosie moaned as they found themselves approaching the hampers. "Oh, look!" she added, as they turned into the Stonehenge enclosure. "Why, Bunny's a fairy godmother. She's waved her wand and, presto, the luncheon appeared!"

Together Bunny and Zeke had brought out the big, rough table from the cabin and the even rougher chairs which furnished it. But a many-colored paper cloth covered the imperfections of the table. On it were paper plates, mugs, cups and saucers. A huge bunch of bayberry filled a pitcher in the center, looking, Silva said, "exactly like a Japanese print."

On the table also were piled platefuls of sandwiches—not the tiny, pretty ones the girls of the Big Eight made when Bunny entertained guests, but triangularly shaped big ones, with lamb or beef or ham between the slices of buttered bread. There were olives, angel cake, big round sugar cookies and shelled nuts. There was iced coffee, iced milk and ginger ale.

How Bunny and Robin and Zeke ate! How Scrab ate! How Midge ate! How the Big Eight ate!

XIV

The Last Straw

THE AFTERNOON started out beautifully. After they had rested a bit from their tremendous luncheon, Robin said, "How about Northern Eye?"

Sitting on the grass, Arthur leaped to his feet in one motion. "I can't wait to see Northern Eye," he announced.

In a moment, they were off, Robin wheeling Scrab as before. For a while, the road—hugging the shore as had the road to Southern Eye—seemed almost the duplicate of that road. Then it began to get rougher. Great rocks jutting out of the sand tore the oncoming waves to foaming pieces and then ground them to drops. Presently—

"Listen, Scrab," Arthur called. "Do you hear something?"

Everyone stopped and froze to voicelessness and movelessness.

116

"I hear a noise," Scrab answered sullenly, "like a gun."

"That's it," Arthur assured him. "That's the Spout!"

The sound grew louder and louder. Presently they were upon it. Back into the island extended a round funnel, dug out by the waters from the solid rock. The waves, bursting into this long, narrow pipe, boomed their protest all along its length and then, still booming, poured back onto the sand.

They stood there for a while watching and listening. The Big Eight, much excited by their beloved Spout, broke into admiring phrases and adjectives.

Scrab said nothing.

They walked on farther and soon they were rounding the curve of the northern coast of Northern Eye and proceeding across the island. Presently they turned into another road which ran southward. This, Robin informed Scrab, took them back to Stonehenge. They passed a pond, twin to the pond on Southern Eye.

"Scientists," Robin explained, "think that these two islands are the tops of twin extinct volcanoes and the two ponds are what were once the craters."

Midge listened, round-eyed. Scrab said nothing.

"Tell Scrab and Midge your adventure, Arthur!" Bunny suggested.

"It was the time we spent the week end on Spectacles," Arthur complied at once. "We all went for a walk on Northern Eye. I saw something strange there, but I didn't really know I saw it. It was just as though my mind took a picture without my knowing. In the morning when I woke up, I remembered it. I had asked Mr. Westabrook if I could get up early and take a walk on Northern Eye. He said I could any time, so that morning I did."

"What did you notice?" Scrab demanded rudely.

"I'm coming to that," Arthur answered quietly. "I had noticed it without—without—"

"Noting," Robin supplied the word.

"That's it—without noting it," Arthur said gratefully. "I saw a great long streak in the high grass, as though something—not big but flat and long—had been crawling there. I felt frightened, but I wanted to know what it was. So I climbed a tree and waited. After a long while, something I could not see came toward me moving through the grass. Pretty soon I saw that it was a great anaconda—oh, it was about fifteen feet long."

"An anaconda's a big snake, isn't it?" Scrab asked.

"Yes," Robin answered. "Go on, Arthur!"

"It was coming straight towards me," Arthur went on, "and by this time I was good and scared. I almost wished I hadn't come. Anyway, I wished I had told Robin about it and asked him to come with me. But there I was up the tree and I didn't know whether great serpents climbed trees or not. Then I remembered that they *did*. And then was I terrified!"

The Big Eight laughed heartlessly at Arthur's panic. Arthur laughed too.

"Well, fortunately, the serpent turned off and went

towards the pond. And then did I scramble down out of that tree and head for the Stone House! Boy, I did it in one minute flat!

"Well, Mr. Westabrook was there and three other grownups and the rest of the Big Eight. At first no one would believe me. But after I had told my story clear through, Robin believed me. Robin said we must capture the anaconda. He knew just how to do it, too. He'd helped to capture serpents in South America. So we got a long board and plenty of rope, and went back to Northern Eye."

"Don't forget we girls sat in a tree," broke in Rosie. "You think you were frightened, Arthur Brine! You don't know what the word *frightened* means. I *do*."

Everyone laughed as they always did at Rosie. Arthur went on.

"Mr. Anaconda was fast asleep when we found him. He looked like a thick, rusty-iron waterpipe, all coiled up. And there was a fat bulge somewhere along his length where he'd just swallowed a big bird whole. Well, Robin prodded Mr. Anaconda until he woke up and started off, and then we formed in a file beside him. Robin had had the grownups cut eight strong forked sticks. Robin counted one-two-three and then, just like a machine, we all reached down and pinned him down with the forked sticks. Then, one after another, we got hold of him."

"I can remember just how he felt," exclaimed Harold. "What strong muscles he had and how he squirmed!"

"We stretched him out on the board and tied him

onto it. Then we carried him to Stonehenge. We found out later that he had escaped from a boat bringing big game back from South America. We sent him up to Boston the next day, and his owners claimed him."

"What a wicked-looking head he had!" exclaimed Dicky. "Boy!"

"And such cruel eyes!" shuddered Laura.

"That was a real adventure," Robin commented.

Scrab said nothing.

Ignoring Scrab utterly and talking among themselves, the Big Eight followed Robin as he wheeled Scrab back to the cabin. Zeke had, in the meantime, burned up the paper table fittings and had packed the empty bottles and pitchers in the hampers.

"It's half-past four," Robin declared, looking at his wrist watch. "The captain said he'd be back for us at five. It will take us about a half an hour to make it to the pier."

They set off. So nicely had Robin calculated that the launch had just moored when they arrived. They sailed back over a sea pulled as taut as a canvas painted rose and azure. The sun, sliding downward between bars of pink and blue clouds, was still far above the horizon.

They found a welcoming Granny and a welcoming Mrs. Dore awaiting them, and a delicious hot fish chowder for supper.

"Before we go to bed," Arthur said, "let's walk down to the Magic Mirror. I want to see if it's still there," he added quizzically.

Robin smiled. "Apparently you haven't had enough walking today, Big Eight," he commented.

"I think I won't go with you," Midge decided, as the Big Eight gathered outside on the lawn. "I've had three walks today and I guess that's enough. I'll sit here and talk with Scrab until you come back."

"What would you like us to bring you back from the far country we're going to explore?" Maida asked.

"Bring me—" Midge paused and reflected. "A great big pearl," she went on, "a nightingale in a golden cage, and—and—a pond lily and a baby fawn."

"You shall have them all," Maida assured Midge gaily. "What would you like, Scrab?"

"Nothing," Scrab said venomously, "except a pair of earmuffs, so I can't hear all the silly talk that's going round here."

Paralyzed for a moment, no one of the Big Eight spoke. Then, as in one movement, they wheeled, marched across the road and onto the path that led to the Bosky Dingle.

Alone with Midge, Scrab said, still venomously, "I guess I gave them something to talk about that time."

"Scrab," Midge said hotly, "I think you are the rudest boy I ever saw in my life. I should think you'd be ashamed of yourself, treating these people who have been so kind to you, the way you do."

"I treat them the way I feel towards them," Scrab answered shrilly. "I hate them all, every one of them." He paused and added weakly, "except Delia."

"You hate Granny Flynn and Mrs. Dore?" Midge asked in a tone of horror.

"Sure I do," Scrab sneered.

"You hate Bunny and Robin?" Midge asked as one not believing her own words.

"Sure I do," Scrab sneered again.

"You hate the Big Eight?" Midge stared white-faced at Scrab.

"Sure I do!" And now Scrab spat on the lawn. "I hate them worst of all."

"Scrab!" Midge began passionately. She stood up. Rage flared in her face. The light from the setting sun shone full in her brown eyes, lighted fires there. Her red hair seemed to lick the air with flames. "I won't stay here and listen to such ingratitude. You are the most dreadful person I ever knew in my life."

"You ought to see my Uncle Ed," Scrab cackled. "Believe me, he's— But you don't have to stay here and talk to me. I didn't ask you. It was your idea. But before you go, I'd like to say a few things to *you*, Miss Midge Golightly—"

Midge's eyes flashed now with the rage of courage. "Go on, Scrab!" she dared him. "Say anything you want! But do you think I'd pay any attention to a— a—a skunk like you?"

"So I'm a skunk, am I?"

Scrab burst into a sudden shout of sarcastic laughter. But he silenced it suddenly, turned back to see if anyone in the Little House had heard it. Apparently no one had. No figure appeared at a door, no face at a window.

"All right, Miss Midge Golightly, I'm a skunk. Well, you're a toady! Do you know what a toady is?"

And at Midge's puzzled stare, he went on. "No, you don't. But I do. I looked it up in the dictionary. It means a fawning flatterer. I may be a skunk, but *that's* what you are—a fawning flatterer. You don't like these people any more than I do. But you're a toady. You fawn on them. You flatter them. You keep telling them how nice they are and how kind they are, and how sweet they are!"

Scrab's voice made something dreadful of the words, *nice, kind, sweet.*

"Of course I tell them those things," Midge replied, "because I mean them. No one in my whole life has ever been so nice and kind and sweet to me. No one has ever—"

"Baloney!" Scrab interrupted. "You don't mean a word you're saying. I know it and you know it. You're just a little toady, buttering these people up, so they'll adopt you and keep you here and never send you away."

For an instant, white-faced and flashing-eyed, Midge stared at Scrab. She opened her mouth to answer him. And then—it was as though Scrab's cruel words had opened a vein in her composure, and it all flowed away.

"I do not," she began. And then suddenly she began to sob. "You are telling dreadful lies about me, Scrab. I won't stand it." Her voice grew hysterical. It rose to a scream. "I won't stand it, I tell you! It's all a lie!"

Figures appeared at the doors and windows of the Little House fast enough now. Florabel, Poppy, Della,

Zeke crowded the kitchen entrance. Mrs. Dore, in an upper window, stared out terrified. Bunny and Robin rushed onto the lawn from the New Ell.

"What's going on here?" Robin demanded sternly. "What have you been saying to Midge, Scrab?"

"He said I—he said I—he called me a—" But Midge's breath gave out as her sobs grew louder.

"I'll take of Midge, Robin," Bunny said, "if you'll take care of Scrab. I'll put her in the guest room to-night, so that she can rest quietly." Bunny put her arm about the sobbing little girl and drew her gently into the house and upstairs. Midge's sobs ran down under Bunny's gentle treatment. But she said nothing. Only an occasional long, breathy sigh told that she was still upset.

In the meantime, the Big Eight, returning from the Magic Mirror, heard the screams, rushed back to the Little House. They arrived in time to witness the end of this scene. They did not cross the road. They stood in a silent group, mystified and horrified, just where the path through the Bosky Dingle ended.

Robin remained silent, his face set.

Scrab started to speak.

"I'm not going to listen to you until tomorrow, Scrab," Robin said. "I'll help you get to bed now."

He wheeled Scrab back into his room, undressed him in complete silence, lifted him on to the bed. With a curt "Good night!" for a return of which he did not wait, Robin closed the door.

"Midge and Scrab had a talk," he explained to the Big Eight, "and apparently Scrab said something that hurt Midge's feelings. We heard her crying, and Bunny is putting her to bed in the spare room. We want her to sleep. Don't any of you speak to her, please."

The Big Eight replied with confused assents and promises. They went into the living room and talked over the episode of Midge and Scrab. But as they knew really nothing about it, they could engage only in useless conjecture. At nine o'clock, exhausted, not by their picnic, but by Midge's misadventure, they said good night and went to bed.

Alone with his wife, Robin said, "Unless Mr. Westabrook has some other plan, I'm going to recommend sending Scrab back to the Home. We've done everything we could think of for him. I've stood more than I've told you about, Bunny. But when it comes to tongue-lashing a little girl until she has hysterics— *that* is the last straw!"

Bunny said, "Mr. Westabrook is away. When does he come back?"

"Tomorrow, I think," Robin answered. "I'll get him on the telephone as soon as I can."

XV

Scrab and Delia

An atmosphere of tension, as thick as a pall of smoke after a fire, hung over the Little House the next morning. At the breakfast table, the silence was complete, except when Bunny or Robin broke it to say, "Please pass the sugar!" "Please pass the butter!" Remarks, equally unimportant, passed among the Big Eight. Midge was now perfectly composed, but silent, unsmiling. Scrab, leaden-faced and icy-eyed, spoke to no one. He asked neither for the sugar nor the salt; the cream nor the butter.

"Boys, I'm going to ask you to stay in the gym this morning," Robin said as he arose from the table, "for I may need you later. You girls might as well go swimming as usual. But please stay at the Magic Mirror until I come after you."

The Big Eight recognized that these pleasant suggestions were commands. Immediately after the chores were done, the boys streamed into the gym.

The girls, in their bathing suits, made for the Magic Mirror. Robin wheeled Scrab onto the lawn with a brief "I'm coming out to talk with you after a while, Scrab," and then disappeared into the New Ell. Granny Flynn appeared with Delia in her arms. "This young lady has been calling for 'my Sab' all the morning. Will you moind her, Scrab?"

"Sure, Granny Flynn," Scrab answered.

Scrab took a magazine from the table. He fluttered the leaves for a moment. Then he put it back on the table. Delia toddled over to his side. She lifted her hands high and answering her signal, Scrab lifted her onto his lap. "My Sab!" she exclaimed radiantly. "My Sab. Delia love her Sab!" She repeated, with an accent on the word, "Delia *love* Sab!"

"How much do you love me, Delia?" Scrab asked in a low voice. "Show me!"

The answer to this question was one of Delia's little tricks. She stretched her arms as wide as she could stretch them. Scrab looked about him hastily. There was no one in sight. He bent his head and kissed the tangle of red curls that covered Delia's head. Then he heaved a sigh so long and so deep that any grown person, hearing it, would have looked at him in alarm. Delia, of course, paid no attention to it.

Scrab lifted Delia off his lap and placed her on the ground. "Play with your dollies, Delia," he ordered gently. Delia toddled over to the spot where lay Baby, her favorite doll, a shapeless rag creation whose face was a blank because Delia had kissed all its painted features off, and Mary, a little plastic girl, blue-eyed and with smiling red lips, who always accompanied Delia to her bath.

Scrab took up another magazine and put it back. He lay back in his chair and looked about him.

It was another of the brilliant sunny days that had marked the summer. Above surged great clouds, as light as foam, but as thick as snow, all swirled and whirled into fantastic mountainous shapes. Through the trees across the way, Scrab could see between the green leaves squares and ovals and triangles of sky. A robin, dropping his gay, musical salute, flew past. A pair of butterflies, their wings beating so close that they might have been tied together, came floating across the lawn.

Everyone in the Little House was busy with morning work. Doorways and windows were empty. No voice sounded. The barn door was open. No sound came from the barn. What could the boys be doing that kept them so quiet, Scrab wondered. Perhaps they were speeding through the air on the traveling rings. A sudden longing flooded over him. Scrab thought how much he would like to skim through the air. He put his hands up to his face as though he were about to cry. And then, his eyes hardening to ice, his face turning to lead, he dropped his hands.

How quiet it was! No sound but the faint patter of the leaves as the breezes rushed through them, and Delia's whispery monologue as she talked to her dolls: "Baby be dood! Mary be dood! Delia spank if dollies be bad!"

And then suddenly, Scrab heard—far away at first

—a faint pounding on the road as of heavy hoofs. What could it be? There were no horses about. Scrab sat up straight and then leaned forward, turning an ear to the sound. It was coming closer, getting louder, fiercer. Suddenly, Scrab heard a bellow.

And then he knew!

And now he could see! King Solomon was speeding towards the Little House. He was in a raging temper. The breath that came from his flaring nostrils was like steam. How he was racing! Scrab's heart contracted. What should he do? What could he do? *Delia!*

All these thoughts raced through Scrab's mind in a second.

And then suddenly he found what he could do!

He leaped from his chair, scooped Delia up into his arms and made for the barn, all the time calling at the top of his voice, "Help! Help! Help! Close the door after me!"

He could see Dicky appear with his hand on the door. Scrab flashed through the door, which shut behind him, shut so close to the bull's head that it almost grazed the steaming nostrils. Scrab put Delia carefully down and then sank to the floor beside her.

"You saved my sister's life, Scrab!" Dicky exclaimed huskily, picking Delia up. "How can I ever thank you?"

"Gee, Scrab, you showed presence of mind," Harold said admiringly. "If you had gone to any of the other doors, the bull would have got you."

"And what presence of mind to call 'Close the door

after me!' " Arthur said. "We were all ready for you."

"Scrab!" Tyma exclaimed. And Tyma screamed it. "You ran. You ran! You're not lame any longer. You're cured. You *ran!*"

Scrab repeated almost stupidly after him, "I ran. I ran. I'm not lame any longer. I'm cured."

Then, curiously enough, it was Scrab who took charge of the situation. "Let's go upstairs," he said, "and watch them catch the bull."

Arthur took one of Scrab's arms and Tyma took the other, but Scrab walked up the stairs. Dicky followed with Delia.

And now the silence of the day was rent with voices.

"Don't come out of the barn, boys!" Robin called from his window in the New Ell. "King Solomon is still here. Scrab," he added, "I can't tell you how I admire your quick thinking. And you ran to the barn as though you'd been running all summer!"

Robin did not say that that was what the doctors had said—that Scrab could walk, and would walk, when he *had* to walk. "I guess I wasn't so brave as you think, Robin," Scrab replied. "You see, I was saving my own life too. But I did think more of Delia."

Came Granny's quavering voice, "Oh, my dear lad, how I bless you! I'll pray to all the saints for you and I'll pray ivery night."

Came Mrs. Dore's voice. "I can't say anything, Scrab. My heart is too full. But I'm her mother, and I guess you know how I feel."

At Mrs. Dore's words, "I'm her mother. I guess you know how I feel," a strange look came across Scrab's face. Sadness shadowed it deeply. His eyes turned dead. But he answered at once. "Sure, I know how you feel, Mrs. Dore."

All the time, their fierce visitor, who now had retreated to the road, was pawing the ground with a fierce front hoof. He looked here and there, following the voices, as though he were trying to find someone on whom to vent his rage.

"The girls!" Bunny suddenly exclaimed in a voice of terror.

"They won't come back to the house," Robin reassured his wife. "I told them when they left to stay at the Magic Mirror until I came for them. They'll wait!"

"Oh yes, if you told them to," Bunny agreed. "The darlings!"

Hubbub sounded on the road. There appeared first Mr. Maybury in his rattling old Ford.

"We're all right, Mart," Robin called. "Scrab and Delia were out on the lawn, but Scrab, suddenly finding out that he could walk, ran with Delia to the barn."

"You don't tell me!" Mart Maybury answered. "Wait till I tell Elvira. She's worried almost to death."

"I'll telephone her," Bunny called. She disappeared from the window.

"How'd he get out?" Robin asked.

"Hasp on the door broke," Mart answered.

"How you going to get him back, Mr. Maybury?" Mrs. Dore asked.

"Oh, they'll get him back, all roight," Granny answered her daughter. "You just wait."

There appeared on the road Mart's assistant, Si Jacks, leading a cow.

At sight of the cow, all King Solomon's hatred of the human race seemed to evaporate. He moved over towards her. Si Jacks urged the cow forward. The bull took a placated position back of her, and in a file, Si leading Madame Cow, King Solomon following her, the antiquated Ford still holding Mart Maybury, the procession disappeared.

"A bull will always folley a cow," said Granny Flynn.

"We'll be back up here later," Mart called.

The instant the coast was clear, all the occupants of the Little House swarmed onto the lawn. Mrs. Dore seized her little daughter and rained kisses on her. Then she passed her to Granny, who duplicated the performance. They they both hugged and kissed Dicky.

"Wait a minute! I wasn't in any danger," Dicky protested.

But Granny and Mrs. Dore paid no attention to him—they were too busy kissing Scrab. Dicky had blushed and struggled under the embraces of his mother and grandmother. But Scrab not only did not struggle or protest. He actually returned their hugs.

The kitchen crew returned to their work. But no one else would go back into the house.

"Robin, don't you think you'd better get the girls?" Bunny said after a while.

"I've been thinking of that," Robin answered. "But in the meantime let's arrange a little surprise for them. How do you feel, Scrab?"

"Great, sir," Scrab answered, "stronger than King Solomon."

"Well then," Robin answered, "when I appear with the girls, I want you to get up and walk towards them with your hands out. Do you suppose you can do it?"

Scrab's green eyes actually reflected Robin's twinkle. "I'm sure I can."

Robin hurried over the path to the Bosky Dingle. The group on the lawn did not say a word. They listened for the sound of approaching girls. Suddenly they heard voices and, as suddenly, the girls appeared.

Scrab arose from his chair, and, his hand extended, walked steadily across the lawn and across the road.

The girls stopped, as though in an instant they had been turned to marble.

"Welcome home!" Scrab greeted them.

Rosie broke from the group, rushed to Scrab and threw her arms about him. The other three girls followed, and for a moment it looked as though Scrab was going to be smothered in embraces.

And this time he did blush—furiously.

XVI

The New Scrab

SCRAB WALKED into the dining room the next morning, just as Midge had. His appearance was greeted with applause. Scrab blushed as the handclapping kept up, but he smiled. Indeed, for the whole day the smile was never far from Scrab's lips. Before he left the table, he said, "I would like to say something to you, to all of you, please."

Mrs. Dore and Granny had half risen to leave the dining room, but immediately they sank back into their seats.

"I've been a—a crumb," Scrab began, "and I know it. I knew all the time just how bad I was being, but I couldn't stop myself from being bad. I'll try to explain—"

Scrab paused, and a baffled look came into his eyes. But they cleared and he went on.

"When I think of it, there's no excuse for me being such a—" Scrab paused to look with a smile at Midge —"skunk."

"Oh, Scrab," Midge protested. "I'm sorry I called you that."

"I'm not," Scrab said. "I was a skunk. But you see, there were two things that made me one. Once I loved someone and that person treated me like—like a—" Scrab's lips formed the word *dog*, but his voice refused to utter it. "So I said to myself I would never love anyone again as long as I lived. I made a resolution to hate everybody. I tried to hate you—all of you. But I couldn't. That only made me try harder. But I couldn't hate you. I said to myself, 'If I can't hate them, I can act as though I did hate them.' That's why I did such—" Scrab appeared to be hunting for an adjective to describe the dreadfulness of his conduct, but he gave it up. "That's why I said such—" Again he searched for an adjective. Again he gave it up.

"But I *wanted* to do everything you asked me to do. I *wanted* to learn all the things you said you'd teach me. In my heart, I liked you all."

He paused. Every face at the table looked understandingly and pityingly at him. The fires in Rosie's black eyes were put out by her tears.

Scrab paused and thought.

"Scrab," Maida began.

"Wait, Maida, just a moment, please," Scrab went steadily on. "I am trying to think of all the things I want to say to you. I thought I was never going to walk again. I thought I was going to spend all my life in a wheelchair. The doctors told me to try to walk. But I couldn't try. I wanted to walk and yet I could not try. So that's the way it was," he concluded.

Robin spoke first. "We all understand, Scrab. So you need never say another word of this. And now," he added briskly, "since Scrab can walk as well as the best of you, although perhaps not yet as far as you can, you take him wherever he wants to go."

What a day followed!

First of all, with lightning speed, the Big Eight did the chores.

"Young fellow, you'll be doing this with us in another week," Arthur warned Scrab. Then they got into swimming shorts and walked down to the Magic Mirror. Scrab said he wanted to walk, too. And Scrab did walk to the Magic Mirror.

"Is the view as good from your own feet as from a wheelchair?" Dicky asked.

"Oh, much better!" Scrab said. "The sky looks bluer and the sunshine goldener and the trees greener." He bent down and laid the palm of his hand flat on the earth. "How good it feels!" he said as though to himself.

Scrab did not engage in the race into the water with which, always, the Big Eight began their swim. But once in, he showed himself to be a swimmer. His head low, his slim body cutting the water like a blade, he made such swift progress that Arthur growled, "You stop that, boy, or you'll take my championship away from me."

But when he reached the first raft, Scrab climbed up and sat on it, resting while he watched the others go through their various stunts.

They stayed all the morning at the Magic Mirror.

But on the way back, Scrab asked to see House Rock and the Fairy Ring.

In the afternoon, Robin suggested that Scrab take his usual nap. But Scrab declared that he had never felt better. At Scrab's request, they climbed up into the Tree Room. Scrab examined Spectacles Island with the binoculars. "There was another story beside the one about the serpent," he reminded them. "Tell it to me now."

And, so, one beginning, a second taking it up here, a third carrying it on there and all interrupting, the Big Eight told Scrab how their scow, *The Ark*, with all the Big Eight aboard, had pulled loose from its moorings, floated off and had stranded all the Big Eight on Spectacles Island.

"We had to stay there until the storm stopped," Rosie said. "'That night we had for dinner nothing but what was left of our luncheon. I melted some chocolate bars and made a funny kind of drink."

"It tasted good," Tyma said. "And it was hot."

"Oh, how cold we were!" Maida recalled.

"Mr. Westabrook had blankets and food dropped to us by airplane," Harold contributed. "That was an adventure that *was* an adventure."

On their way back to the lawn, the Big Eight took Scrab to the rear of the Little House, so that he could walk through the two big plots, the vegetable and the flower garden.

"Look at it hard, Scrab!" Harold advised him. "In a day or two you'll be helping us clean it up for the winter. And will that break your back!"

"I want to help," Scrab said. He added, "And do you think, some afternoon, we could walk up the road to Mr. Maybury's farm to see King Solomon?"

"Do you mean to tell me," Rosie broke out in a scandalized voice, "that you want to see that dreadful bull again?"

"Yes, I do," Scrab admitted.

"Come to think of it, that isn't so strange," Rosie confessed, "because I'd like to see him again myself. I hope they've put a good strong lock on the door, though."

After luncheon, Scrab asked the Big Eight if they would show him the Map Room and the library. Delighted at his interest, for now that interest was warm and genuine, they spent part of the afternoon in the one and part in the other. Scrab examined the maps interestedly. He read the titles of books here and there; occasionally took a volume off the shelf and examined it.

"Now I can come in here," he exclaimed jubilantly, "and pick out stories for myself."

"That's what we all do," Maida informed him.

"Scrab has never been upstairs," Silva remembered. "Let's show him our rooms and Granny's and Mrs. Dore's."

Scrab said, "I want to see everything."

And so upstairs they scrambled. Scrab looked at the girls' rooms with as civil and polite an air as he could summon.

"After this," he suddenly exclaimed, "if Bunny

and Robin will let me, I'd like to sleep in the barn with you fellows."

"They'll let you," Maida assured him.

Scrab's arrival in the big, comfortable living room of the grownups' department created excitement. Delia, spying him first, ran to him, calling, "My Sab! My Sab!" She lifted her arms high. Scrab picked her up and held her.

They saw Granny Flynn's sunny little bedroom, as bare as a nun's but for her *Book of the Saints*, which lay on a table beside her bed with her place marked by her rosary; the framed pictures of her grandchildren and the Big Eight. They saw Mrs. Dore's pretty room, a little gayer with pictures and bric-a-brac. They saw the nursery where Delia and Nesta slept. The wallpaper was divided into panel scenes in color, from *Mother Goose*. Low shelves held toys. There were two low beds; two low tables with tiny chairs—one set painted blue and the other pink. A big roomy closet contained two bureaus.

After dinner, the Big Eight indulged in singing. And what with Dicky's violin, Scrab's harmonica— not to mention Bunny's improvised accompaniment on the piano—and the lusty voices of the young people, the house should have shaken with the force of the music. Yet, upstairs the two little girls slept peacefully through it.

"Now," Maida announced as they went to bed, "we're the Big Ten."

It was as though one Scrab had left the house and

another Scrab had taken his place. The new Scrab was a completely different boy, quiet, gentle, modest, trying his best to help in every way, doing his best to join in all their activities. The Big Eight sometimes looked at each other in astonishment.

Once Rosie said, "I feel as though all that time we hated Scrab was a dream."

And Maida answered, "Let's pretend it was a dream."

What touched most of all the warm, generous hearts of the Big Eight was that Scrab remembered all the offers they had made to entertain him when he first came to the Big House. Shyly, he asked questions in regard to them.

And so it came about that on rainy days he spent long sessions with Harold and his stamp collection. He examined the stamps as Harold directed, through the magnifying glass that Harold had bought for just that purpose. Their study was interrupted by frequent visits to the Map Room to look up the countries from which the stamps had come, the very names of which were unknown to Scrab.

"Say, Harold, you know all these countries," Scrab suggested, "and I'm going to learn them, too. But while I'm about that, let's learn the capital cities of every country in the world!"

Harold agreed to this suggestion. It turned out to be, in some ways, an easier task than they expected and, in others, a harder one. Finally Scrab suggested that they make duplicate lists of these important cities. Harold begged the use of Bunny's typewriter for an afternoon and after a long session with the atlas, the geography and the maps in the Map Room, they produced two lists, rather imperfectly typed but geographically correct.

Scrab tried his best to learn from Dicky how to play the violin. But after a while, he admitted defeat. "I haven't got something that you've got," he explained his dilemma to Dicky. "I don't know what, exactly. I guess perhaps I haven't the ear for violin music. But I tell you what let's do. Let's work up some duets, you on the fiddle and me on the harmonica."

The idea of this delighted Dicky. They did all their practicing outside, and whenever a weird wail or a hollow hoot rang from the surrounding woods, everyone in the Little House smiled. "They're at it again!" someone was sure to say.

Often Scrab walked with Tyma and tried his hardest to learn the lore of the woods from him. "Gee, I didn't see that," he would exclaim in self-disgust when Tyma pointed out to him tree scars; a blaze high up on a tree trunk; two pairs of initials, carved within the outline of a heart, fast swelling out of shape; a bit of delicate moss growing on a boulder; a discarded snake skin; a satiny piece of birch bark; a tightly rolled fern just beginning to unfurl; a gliding snake; darting squirrels. And once, in a pasture—casually—Tyma stooped down and picked up an Indian arrowhead which he presented to his awed companion.

"Your eyes just eat up the ground!" Scrab said.

By this time of course, Scrab had moved into the barn. The gym was tirelessly fascinating to him. The boys of the Big Ten were his tutors here. They taught him to use the traveling rings and the chest weights, how to carry the canoe to the Magic Mirror and how to balance himself, how to paddle it. And Robin taught him to fence.

However, at one sport, Scrab was master—boxing! No one of the other boys was so fast, so powerful, so elusive.

"It's like trying to punch a ghost!" Arthur complained.

Except for Maida, the girls could do little for Scrab. "Of course I could teach you how to cook," Rosie suggested playfully. "But I know what any boy would say to that. NO! He'd be afraid he'd have to cook if he knew how."

At first Scrab declined—although good-naturedly —Rosie's offer. But later he said, "Maybe one day I'll take you up on that offer, Rosie, to teach me to cook. Suppose we all went camping, as they're talking about doing, it would come in pretty handy to be able to get a meal."

"We'd all have indigestion!" Arthur hooted.

The boys burst into derisive laughter. But Robin, reading his paper, interrupted to say quietly, "I can cook. How many times, hunting in South America and Africa, was I glad that I could!"

The laughter of the boys came to a sudden stop. "Gee, I never thought of that," Arthur said.

Scrab did not ask Silva to teach him to paint. But

he often watched, fascinated, when she sat by the Magic Mirror. "When you see a picture," he commented once, "it looks so easy. But when I watch you, I realize how hard it is."

Maida, as she most humbly admitted, could teach Scrab little. But Scrab was a great reader and so was Maida. They engaged in endless talks about books. It happened that Maida was not one of those girls who likes to read only books about girls. She read almost as many boys' as girls' books. And Scrab was not one of those boys who will read only books about boys. He read almost as many girls' as boys' books. Obviously, with both of them, it was the story that counted most.

But Scrab did remind Laura that she had offered to dance for him.

Tyma suggested that they make up a Fairy Ring party, "And you put on a show for us, Laura."

Laura assented and the afternoon was set. All the morning, Laura, assisted by Midge and Rosie, was lugging costumes down to the Fairy Ring, concealing them in the near-by clump of bushes which was her dressing room.

At luncheon, Bunny and Robin asked if they could go to the "show." And when Laura assented enthusiastically, Granny Flynn and Mrs. Dore petitioned to be part of the audience.

"Why don't we invite Florabel and Polly and Della and Zeke to come?" Bunny suggested.

The kitchen crew were delighted. They even dressed in their best for it.

And so, after the boys had brought reclining chairs for the grownups to the border of the Fairy Ring, the audience assembled.

Laura had to dance without music, as neither Dicky nor Scrab knew any dance music. But between groups of dances, the two boys played duets that were actually new to the inhabitants of the Little House.

First, in her Scottish costume, Laura danced a Highland fling and a sword dance.

Second, in misty floating draperies, her hair hanging in waving masses, a crown of flowers on her head, she danced a fairy dance.

Third, dressed like a gob, she danced the Sailor's Hornpipe.

Last, she danced two dances that she had made up herself. One was the Giraffe Dance, the other the Hippopotamus Dance. The giraffe was dignified, in spite of the lolloping gait which Laura had copied from giraffes themselves. But the hippopotamus was as lumbering and awkward as a "refrigerator on wheels," Tyma said. The kitchen crew particularly enjoyed this. And so the exhibition ended on laughter that was both loud and long.

But it soon became evident to the people of the Little House that, although it was a new Scrab who was living with them, it was a boy subject to periods of intense unhappiness. Of this anguish, Scrab never spoke. Nor did the Big Eight. But they soon began to recognize the blank bleak look that came into Scrab's face at the return of his heartbreak. Indeed, sometimes his eyes were so filled with suffering that, on one excuse or another, the rest of the Big Ten left him to the solitude they knew he wanted.

Everyone noticed these seizures. Although the grownups must have discussed it among themselves, they never mentioned the subject to the young people.

But the Big Eight talked it over many times.

"It must be that person who treated him so badly," Dicky said once, "that he's thinking of. I wonder who it was."

"Scrab's body is well again," Silva said, "but his heart is still lame."

The summer days slipped by. And then one day Bunny and Robin drove in the car to Boston, and were gone a night and two days.

XVII

"Mom"

L<small>ET'S</small> <small>ALL</small> sit out on the lawn for a while," Bunny suggested, the morning after she and Robin came home.

"But what about the chores, Bunny?" Rosie asked.

"Let's forget the chores for once," Bunny replied. "I've been away from you for two days and I've forgotten how you look."

The Big Ten laughed at this. Harold remarked, "It's wonderful how willing I am to put off doing the chores!"

"You sit here, Scrab," Bunny said, pointing to a long, low reclining chair which faced the road in the direction of the Big House. "And Maida there, and you—" Just as though she were setting the scene for an act, Bunny indicated where they all were to place themselves. Finally the four grownups settled themselves in the comfortable armchairs. "Now what shall we talk about, Big Ten?" Bunny asked. And sud-

denly all her dimples were exploding like fireworks in
her charming little face.

"What was the most *terrifying* adventure you had
in Boston, Bunny?" Maida asked.

Bunny answered instantly. "Well, yesterday I got
up early to take a walk on the Public Garden," she
began. Her eyes went to Scrab's face and stayed
there.

Scrab's face had the frozen look which always
came over it when unhappiness settled upon him. He
had closed his eyes.

Bunny kept her gaze on him.

"It was so early that there was no one in the Garden but me," Bunny continued. "It was a sweet scene,
the birds all practicing the music they were going to
sing that day, the trees all shaking the dust out of
their leaves and the flowers all spraying the air with
perfume. Well, I had come to the pier where they
keep the swanboats. Just a little distance off was a
clump of bushes. And as I approached that clump of
bushes, a lion leaped out and stood lashing his tail and
growling at me."

"Tchk! Tchk!" commented Arthur. "Such rude-
ness!"

"The idea of his growling at you, Bunny!" inter-
posed Rosie indignantly. "You had just as much right
to walk in the Public Garden as he had!"

"What did you do, Bunny," Silva asked, "put salt
on his tail?"

"No," said Bunny. "Somehow I had a feeling that
I did not want to get too close to the lion—he looked

so hungry. I leaped into one of the swanboats and paddled into the middle of the pond. And from there I gave the lion a talking-to."

"What did he say to that, the disagreeable thing!" Maida demanded.

"He said he was awfully hungry. He said he hadn't had any dinner the night before. He said he wanted some breakfast. I told him there were plenty of hotels—" Bunny stopped abruptly.

Scrab had opened his eyes. Suddenly their expression changed.

"What is it, Scrab?" Bunny asked, immediately abandoning her fantastic tale.

"There's a lady walking up the road," Scrab answered hesitantly.

The rest of the Big Ten started to rise, but Robin gestured them back. Mystified, they sat down.

Scrab's gaze was fixed on the road. His look was half-terrified, half-wondering. Slowly he pulled himself upright in his seat and stared at the approaching figure with eyes which had suddenly become big and black.

"Mom!" he screamed suddenly. "Oh, mom! Oh, mom!" He leaped out of his chair, rushed to the road and tore in the direction of the advancing figure.

"Bliss!" the woman answered. "Bliss! Oh, Bliss!"

Scrab raced toward the woman. The woman hurried towards Scrab. They met and their arms went about each other. "You're walking!" the woman sobbed. "They told me you could walk, but I couldn't believe it."

"Oh, mom," Scrab breathed, "is it really you? Have you really come back?"

"It's me, Bliss," the woman answered both questions, "and I've come back."

"So many times, mom, I've dreamed that you came back," Scrab exclaimed. "This isn't a dream, is it, mom?"

"It isn't a dream, Bliss," the woman assured him. She hugged him hard.

"Mom, I thought you'd ratted on me!"

The group on the lawn saw Scrab's face work. His hand went to his trembling mouth. Tears rained down his face.

"I didn't desert you, my darling boy. Your uncle Ed invited me out for a ride in his car. But he never brought me home. He kept on and on until we were way out in the Middle West. I tried to escape, but he watched me every moment. He wouldn't even let me telephone or telegraph. I think he must have lost his mind. And then there was an accident, a truck ran into us. Your uncle Ed was killed. I was thrown clear of the car, but when I regained consciousness, I couldn't remember who I was or where I came from."

"Oh, mom, how I used to think of you! Nights before I fell asleep. Mornings when I woke up! Every little while during the day! But Mrs. Shane, upstairs, told me that you went off in the car with Uncle Ed. I lived in the house as long as there was any food. And then an officer came and took me to a Home. And after a long while, Bunny and Robin came and brought me here. How did you find out where I was? How did you get here? Tell me first, how did you take care of yourself?"

"I did day's work everywhere I could get it, and saved my money. Then one day I was standing on a corner, waiting for traffic to pass. Parked right near me was a car with the driver half asleep. The radio was on. And Bliss, suddenly I heard: 'Attention, Mrs. Bliss Morgan! Attention, Mrs. Bliss Morgan! Your boy is safe, living in the country with friends. Go to the nearest police station and they will see that you get to him.' And, Bliss, that instant, everything came back to me! I asked the way to the police station, and after I had identified myself by showing them my wedding ring with my initials in it, they got on the telephone. It was Mr. Westabrook who was searching for me. Well, the police gave me money and they took me to an airport, and I flew back to Boston. Just think of it, Bliss, I flew! Mr. Westabrook and Bunny and Robin met me there yesterday afternoon, and Bunny went with me and helped me buy these clothes. We didn't get here last night till very late— too late to wake you up."

"Mom! Mom!" Scrab said wildly, "it's like a story in a book. Oh, mom, you did love me! You didn't rat on me. But maybe you're tired now. Come and sit down, mom."

With his arm about his mother, Scrab turned to the little group on the lawn. The tears had been pouring down Scrab's face, and they still poured. But he smiled radiantly as he made awkward, boyish intro-

ductions. "My mom, Big Ten!" he said proudly. And
he named everyone there in turn.

Robin drew up a chair for Mrs. Morgan.

The Big Ten liked her at once. Dark-haired, dark
eyed, her expression was warm and soft, and her big
eyes, warm and soft too, were beautiful. Little hair-
line wrinkles had gathered at the corners of her eyes.
But somehow, they served only to make the expression of those eyes more kind, more loving. She wore
a new linen suit and a little scoop-shaped, pale-yellow
straw hat which was covered over the top with green
leaves, and showed a row of tiny rosebuds under the
brim, close to her face.

Scrab suddenly seemed to become aware of his
mother's appearance. "Mom, you look swell!" he
said proudly.

"I hope you're not tired, Mrs. Morgan," Bunny
said.

"Tired!" Mrs. Morgan answered gaily. "I had
twelve hours sleep last night in the Big House. What
a beautiful place! Why, Bliss, this morning while Mr.
Westabrook and I were having breakfast, peacocks
came walking across the grass, and deer—"

"I've seen them, mom," Scrab boasted radiantly.
"Aren't they just like a picture book?"

Scrab had had to take his arm from about his
mother when she sat down. But he pushed his chair
as close to hers as he could get. And his eyes seemed
to devour her.

Through the window on the second story came the
sound of baby babblings. Mrs. Dore flew upstairs and

returned presently with the two little girls in fresh rompers, their cheeks rosy, their eyes shining after their sleep.

Delia immediately called, "Sab! My Sab!" and held out her arms to Scrab. Scrab immediately lifted her up.

To the amusement of everyone, Nesta, who was as shy as Delia was confiding, held her arms out to Mrs. Morgan, who instantly took her onto her lap. Everyone talked about the children and everyone talked at once.

Suddenly Scrab arose, put Delia gently on Rosie's lap and disappeared. He returned almost immediately with a newspaper parcel in his hands. "Look, mom!" he said. He handed the parcel to his mother.

The Big Eight recognized immediately the package about which Scrab had been so rude the day of his arrival.

It was tied in a hard knot, but Mrs. Morgan broke the string. Inside was a worn, much-darned black sweater.

"My old sweater!" Mrs. Morgan exclaimed. And now the tears poured from her eyes. "You kept it, Bliss!"

"It was all I had to remind me of you, mom," Scrab said. "And now," he continued, a sudden manly note in his voice, "we'll burn it up. You're never going to wear such a raggedy old sweater again. I'm going to work and earn the money to buy you *two* new sweaters!"

"Bliss!" Mrs. Morgan hugged Scrab again.

"Mrs. Morgan, you call Scrab, Bliss," Maida exclaimed.

"That's his name," Mrs. Morgan said. "I never heard this name, Scrab, before."

"The boys in the Home named me that," Scrab explained.

"Why did you let them call you that, son?" his mother asked.

"I didn't care what anybody called me," Scrab said.

"Let's all call you Bliss after this," Maida suggested.

But the household was not very successful in renaming Scrab. Scrab said that he was called Scra-Bliss more often than anything else.

The rest of the Big Ten did their tactful best to leave Scrab and his mother alone. This was indeed a sacrifice on their part, especially for Midge, who tagged Mrs. Morgan wherever she went. They would have liked to accompany the two when Scrab escorted Mrs. Morgan to the Map Room, the Library, the Gym, the boys' sleeping quarters, to the Tree Room, House Rock, the Fairy Ring, in their first walk about the Magic Mirror and on various excursions they took into the thick, deep woods. But if the Big Eight were tactful, so was Mrs. Morgan. She never failed to tell them her impressions of all the charms of the Little House and its attractive surroundings.

But it was not alone the Big Eight with whom Mrs. Morgan was popular. The grownups enjoyed her too. Even the kitchen force, finding out by her delighted appreciation, what food she particularly liked—tomato juice, parsnips, fish chowder, brown Betty—did their best to cater to these tastes. Mrs. Morgan helped Granny Flynn and Mrs. Dore in every way she could. She was always taking the little girls off their hands and—as she was an accomplished seamstress—doing all kinds of mending for them.

"Oh, to think of you darning that rent in me black silk dress!" Granny Flynn exclaimed gratefully. "Sure, I've been trying to make meself do it for weeks. 'Tis the foine, grand woman you are!"

The three ladies sat on the lawn together when it was sunny, and in the upstairs living room when it stormed. But in both places, tongues and fingers flew!

Bunny and Robin delighted in Mrs. Morgan because she was what they called "articulate," meaning that she could describe anything she talked about. She could tell her experiences with the humorous gift—and in many of her stories the thrilling gift—of the born narrator. Not that her language was not simple. But instinctively she picked out details that would most interest her audience. Bunny and Robin never tired of asking her questions about her childhood in Vermont and that forced trip into the Middle West, on which her pugilist brother had taken her. So good was her memory, so acute her observation, so easy her narrative, that her story unrolled like a spool of thread.

After a while, of course, Scrab began to display his new accomplishments to his mother. He and Dicky played duets for her. He and Arthur boxed for her.

He and Harold showed her their stamp collections—
Scrab's very scanty. The two boys recited to her the
capitals of all the countries in the world. But what
seemed to make his mother proudest was an exhibition of which the pair who put it on were completely
unconscious. That was when Maida and Scrab talked
about books. Then, although Mrs. Morgan was wise
enough to make no comment, the joy that filled her
face made it lovely.

One night, as Dicky, tailing the procession of boys
to the barn, started to leave the Little House, Maida
drew him aside. "Dicky," she exclaimed radiantly,
"do you realize that we've cured both our patients?
They can both walk. They're well in body and—"

"Soul," Dicky supplied the word.

XVIII

Parties

M<small>R. WESTABROOK</small> said that he had given them plenty of time to get acquainted with Mrs. Morgan and Mrs. Morgan plenty of time to get acquainted with them. And now, according to the almanac, the summer was really over and the autumn upon them, he proposed that, before it was too late, they have three outdoor parties.

"What kind of parties, father?" Maida asked. "Not that I care!" she hastened to explain. "I like *any* kind of a party."

"Well, first of all," Mr. Westabrook said, "I think you ought to take Mrs. Morgan to Mart Maybury's farm, so that she can see the bull her son outfoxed."

"Oh, Mr. Westabrook," Mrs. Morgan said, "I do want to see that bull. You see, I was brought up on a farm. But more than that, he made my boy walk!"

"They've got a new hasp on the door," Rosie explained. "I met Mr. Maybury on the road and asked him."

"That's Party Number One, father," Maida said. "Now, what's Party Number Two?"

"I thought you'd like to come over to luncheon at the Big House," Mr. Westabrook suggested.

Employing their usual signal of delighted approbation, the Big Ten burst into applause.

"Mr. Westabrook," Rosie pleaded, "couldn't you see some of the deer in the woods and make an engagement with them to cross the lawn that day?"

"I'll do that, Rosie," Mr. Westabrook immediately agreed. "Queer that I've never thought of it before!"

"And Party Number Three, father?" Maida prodded.

"I propose we give Mrs. Morgan a picnic on Spectacles," Mr. Westabrook said.

"Oh, mom," Scrab exclaimed rapturously, "how I've wished that I could explore Spectacles with you!"

"Those are three lovely parties, father," Maida said, her dove eyes shining with happiness.

The Big Ten were particularly delighted with their visit to the Maybury farm. For one thing, they were proud because Mrs. Morgan was such a success.

"Mrs. Morgan and Miss Elvira took to each other at once," Rosie commented afterwards. "But then, who doesn't take to Mrs. Morgan—and to Miss Elvira for that matter? They're both so sweet. And even in her wheelchair, Miss Elvira makes such delicious sugar cookies!"

"My mother makes scrumptious cookies," Scrab boasted.

"Jealous!" Rosie accused him.

It was typical of the change that had come over Scrab that he laughed at Rosie's accusal.

"Mart Maybury liked your mother just as much as Miss Elvira did," Silva put in, "only, being a man, he wouldn't show it so much."

"He certainly did," Maida agreed.

Scrab looked so delighted at this praise of his mother that, "Stop purring, Scra-Bliss!" Laura commanded.

Again Scrab laughed.

Many other pleasant things occurred at the Maybury farm beside Mrs. Morgan's instant popularity.

Of course, the first thing they did was to visit King Solomon. To the Big Ten, he looked quite a different creature. For, after contemplating them for a moment with a lowering, suspicious gaze, he turned back to his feeding. But to Mrs. Morgan, who had been brought up on a farm, and knew how touchy a bull can become, he was alarming.

"To think, Bliss," he said in a daze of wonder, "that you—" She did not finish her sentence, but she patted her son's shoulder.

After their visit to the barn, Mr. Maybury conducted Mrs. Morgan all over the farm. The Big Ten followed them, but Mr. Maybury and Mrs. Morgan engaged in so absorbed a conversation on the contrasts of farming in Vermont and Massachusetts, that after a while the younger members of the party strayed back to the porch. There, Granny Flynn and Mrs. Dore were gossiping with Miss Elvira.

Presently Mrs. Morgan and Mr. Maybury rejoined

them. "This is a fine farm," Mrs. Morgan exclaimed enthusiastically to Miss Elvira, "and so well run. I declare it makes me homesick for my childhood."

"I'm going to work hard, mom," Scrab said, "and save up my money and buy you a farm. Seems to me I'd rather work out of doors where there'd be cows and sheep and pigs and hens—and crops growing—than anywhere else."

"You come naturally by that feeling, Bliss," his mother reminded him. "Remember, you are the last of a long line of farmers."

"Would you like to have a bull on your farm, Scra-Bliss?" Laura asked mischievously.

"I wouldn't be without one," Scrab answered promptly.

"Now I know what to give you for a birthday present," Laura said in a happy tone of voice.

As before, Miss Elvira served cold drinks and some of her delicious Banbury tarts. As before, the girls of the Big Ten timorously invaded the kitchen to ask Myra if they could help. But this time Myra did not even answer them. She put the bottles, glasses and cookies onto the kitchen table and then disappeared into her room, which was just beyond the kitchen, muttering as she went.

However, Myra's ill nature had no effect on the appetites of the five girls. They ate Miss Elvira's tarts until they could eat no more.

The next party, in celebration of Scrab's birthday, was a delightful occasion. For several days, the rest of the Big Ten had been busy with secret prepara-

tions. Yet, when they got into the beach wagon to go
to the Big House, not one of them carried a parcel. At
breakfast they had all given Scrab the appropriate
number of slaps and spanks—gentle on the part of the
girls and tinglingly vigorous on the part of the boys.
Scrab had received them and the good wishes that
accompanied them with a sheepish delight. When
they arrived at the Big House, Mr. Westabrook met
them on the terrace and conducted them indoors.

First of all, Scrab said, "May I show my mother all
the beautiful things I saw here, Mr. Westabrook?"

Mr. Westabrook agreed. Again displaying a sensi-
tive tact, no one of the Big Ten accompanied the two
as Scrab took his mother to the cabinet of "littles,"
to the Meissonier and the Vermeer, to the Strad, to
the great, shining, delicately shaped rose-colored
tropical shell, and to the gigantic, transparent, geo-
metrically shaped turquoise-blue crystal.

After a while the mother and son rejoined the
group on the front terrace.

"Such beautiful things I never did see!" Mrs. Morgan exclaimed.

"Which did you like best, mom?" her son asked
eagerly.

"I guess the picture with those ladies sewing," Mrs.
Morgan answered.

"That would be my choice," Mr. Westabrook
agreed smilingly. "And now let's have luncheon!"

Mr. Westabrook offered Mrs. Morgan his arm and
they led the procession to the terrace at the back.
Mr. Westabrook seated his companion at his right.

To the others, he said, "You'll find place cards where you are to sit."

The Big Ten found their seats swiftly. Scrab found that he was seated beside his mother and that in front of his plate was a pile of parcels. A pretty card tilted against them said, "Happy birthday for Bliss!"

Scrab's eyes grew round with surprise. His cheeks turned red with excitement. "Oh, I didn't think—" he faltered. "You shouldn't have—" he faltered again. He turned in desperation to his mother. "You thank them, mom. I don't know how."

"I've already thanked them, my son," Mrs. Morgan said with wet eyes.

"And I do, too," Scrab took it up. "I thank you all so much that I don't know how to say it."

"Suppose you look at your presents, Bliss," Mr. Westabrook suggested in his kindest manner. "You'll be surprised how the words will come then."

And come the words did—in torrents.

First of all, Scrab opened a big package done up in brown paper and tied with brown cord. On the card was written: *From your pals in the gym.* It was a pair of ice skates.

"Oh!" Scrab exclaimed. "What swell skates! I know how to skate, but I never owned skates of my own. The first day there's ice, I'm going—" Suddenly his face grew serious, almost frightened. "But where'll we be, mom, when winter comes?"

"We'll be where you can skate, son," his mother replied. "I'm sure of that."

Next came two tiny packages, just alike in size and

done up with silver paper and red ribbon. On the tag of one of them was written: *From Bunny, with love and wishes for many happy birthdays!* On the other appeared: *From Robin. A fine birthday this year and many more as good!*

Scrab opened the packages. They contained small, glossy jeweller's boxes. In each box were two big, round, polished silver dollars. "Oh," Scrab exclaimed, "I never had a silver dollar in my life. Thank you, Bunny! Thank you, Robin! Bunny, could I get my mother a new sweater with four dollars?"

"We'll see about that sweater later," Bunny answered with a display of dimples that turned her face into one big sparkle.

His mother patted his shoulder. "Look at your other gifts, Bliss!" she suggested.

The next package, done up in white paper covered with shamrocks, and tied with a green ribbon, was labeled: *From Granny Flynn and Mrs. Dore.* And in it was a knife that—

"Oh, Granny!" Scrab exclaimed ecstatically. "Oh, Mrs. Dore!" He pulled out blade after blade. He pulled out—"A corkscrew!" he exclaimed with delight. He pulled out—"An awl!"

"Why, it's a whole tool chest in itself," Mr. Westabrook commented. "How I would have treasured a knife like that when I was a boy!"

In complete rapture, Scrab sat snapping the sharp, shining blades back and forth.

"Look at your other presents, Bliss!" his mother reminded him.

"I keep forgetting where I am," Scrab murmured. "I never had such a wonderful knife!" He picked up the nearest parcel—a big one. It was a box tied with red, white and blue paper. On the card, which bore a picture of an American eagle, were the words: *From Florabel, Zeke, Poppy and Della. May you live long and prosper!* It was filled with the delicious, round, paper-thin cookies which the Big Ten were always begging Florabel to make.

"Gee!" Scrab exclaimed. "It seems to me I never have eaten enough of those cookies. Now I can."

"If you need assistance," Arthur said graciously, "we boys will help you out."

Scrab laughed. "I'll give you some," he promised, "but I'll watch you every time you put your hand into this box!"

Next came a small, flat envelope, appropriately done up in a paper which had pictures of a little house on it. The card read: *From the girls of the Big Ten.*

Very carefully Scrab slit the flap of the envelope with one of the blades of his new knife. He looked inside. "Oh, gee!" he exclaimed. And then, "Oh, jiminy!" And finally, "Oh, diggety-dog!" He let the contents of the envelope sift onto the tablecloth. "Stamps, mom," he cried, "for my collection! I've only got ten now." He looked them over, reading the strange foreign names. "Oh, girls, what a swell present! I won't be able to say a word to any of you, all day tomorrow. I'll be too busy looking these over."

Very carefully he put the stamps back in the envelope.

But two birthday gifts remained. One, a big one, was done up in gold paper, tied with scarlet ribbon. The card said: *This means work for you. Best wishes! Jerome Westabrook*. Very carefully Scrab untied the scarlet ribbon, took off the gold paper.

"Oh!" he exclaimed. "A stamp album! Oh, Mr. Westabrook, I was saving up for one. Now I won't speak to anyone for a week. I'll be putting my stamps into this book. You'll help me, Harold, won't you?"

"You betcha!" Harold promised.

Last lay a flat envelope. *"Bliss—with love"* was written on the paper in it.

Scrab opened it. Inside, mounted on thick paper, was a photograph of his mother.

Scrab's face crumpled. "Oh, mom!" he said. He put his head on his mother's shoulder. "Oh, how I wished I had a picture of you all that time you were gone!" came from him in stifled accents.

And then Mr. Westabrook produced a diversion. "Look, the deer have come!" he whispered.

But quite as wonderful as Scrab's birthday was the picnic on Spectacles Island.

Afterwards, Harold always referred to it as the "elegant picnic." For, since Mr. Westabrook had proposed it, it followed in every detail Mr. Westabrook's own plan.

When, bubbling with excitement, the party from the Little House—having sailed first across the water to the island and then trekked through the woods to Stonehenge—arrived at the Stone House, they found that someone had preceded them and made the place amazingly attractive and comfortable.

Inside, the cabin had been swept and dusted. Even the windows had been washed. The old stove had been blacked. Outside, a great table had been set on the grass. Camp chairs surrounded it. The beautiful tablecloth was as delicate, the china as thin and the silver as heavy and glittering as though it were a party at the Big House.

"Fairies have been here," Rosie decided. "I'm sure of that. Someone waved a wand and this table appeared—just like in *The Tempest*."

Immediately the Big Eight told Mrs. Morgan of the time they produced *The Tempest*. Mr. Westabrook had transformed an old barn on his place into a summer theater.

"I wish you could have seen Delia and Nesta as baby mermaids," Maida said. "When the curtain went up, they were playing with seashells and seaweed. How the audience applauded them! One of them fell asleep before the act was over. Not that *that* did any harm. It only made it more real."

First of all, they asked Mrs. Morgan if she liked to walk. She declared that she could walk "forever." Immediately they made the round of Northern Eye.

The tide was perfect for a performance from the Spout. All the way, until they reached the scene of Arthur's great adventure, Scrab was pointing out to his mother the beauties of the scene—birds that arrowed through the air in a web of music, flashes of autumn red or yellow in the trees, big, moss-grown boulders and long, low ledges of rock. When they came to the pond on Northern Eye, he asked Arthur to take over. And Arthur, for the second time that summer, described his meeting with the anaconda.

Back at the cabin, they found awaiting them a dinner. "Not a luncheon," Rosie said, "but a dinner and a hot dinner! I never heard of a picnic with a hot meal."

They sat down at the table to glasses filled with cut fruit. Then came steaks, mashed sweet potatoes with a top crust of marshmallows which had been melted and browned, peas, parsnips, ice cream with cake thickly frosted, coffee for the grownups, milk for the Big Ten.

It was so pleasant, sitting in the thick green grass, that they stayed for a long time. The irregular circle of gray boulders gave the place a prehistoric air. The blue cloudless arch of the sky seemed like a glass bowl. The birds, flying constantly over their heads, and producing the gayest of music, might have been their private orchestra.

It was Mr. Westabrook who finally said, "Well, if we're going to Southern Eye, I guess we'd better start."

On that walk, Scrab asked Maida to tell his mother about the time the Ark got shipwrecked on Spectacles. Maida told it with a great deal of help from the rest of the Big Eight, each of whom recalled something that all the others had forgotten. The boys remembered every article of food that the airplane had dropped for them, and the girls remembered the warm sweaters and blankets.

"It's been such a wonderful day!" Mrs. Morgan sighed as they came back to what Rosie described as the "continent of America." "I wasn't brought up by the sea, of course. But I've lived in Boston ever since I married Bliss's father. Oh, how I have enjoyed the sky and the birds and the sunset today! And at the Little House—to hear Mr. Maybury's cocks crowing in the morning and to see his cows in pasture when we pass! It's been beautiful."

No one spoke for a moment.

Then Mr. Westabrook said, "We all know exactly how you feel, Mrs. Morgan."

XIX

Happy Ending

Bᴜᴛ ᴅᴜʀɪɴɢ all this enjoyment, an undercurrent of talk was going on among the girls at the Little House.

"I wonder where Mrs. Morgan and Scrab will go," Silva began it, "after they leave here."

"Oh, I've thought about it so much," Maida sighed. "Mrs. Morgan will have to get a job of some kind, now that her brother is dead. She'll be gone all day and poor Scrab—what will he do?"

"Part of the time he'll go to school, of course," Rosie reminded them.

"But he'll have to cook his own luncheon," Laura said. "And Scrab doesn't know how to cook."

"He'll learn," Maida prophesied. "Scrab is smart."

"But poor Mrs. Morgan will have to cook the dinner after she comes home all tired out," Laura said in a worried tone.

"But Scrab will soon learn to get the vegetables ready and have a kettle of boiling water on the stove and set the table," Maida made prophecy again. "I know he'll learn."

"But all Saturday afternoon and all day Sunday," Silva put in, "poor Mrs. Morgan will have to do mending and sweeping and washing and ironing. I hope they'll go to the movies every Saturday night."

"Scrab will learn to help in all those things," Maida insisted steadily. "He will do anything for his mother. I think I never saw a boy who loved his mother so much."

Quick tears dimmed the brilliancy of Rosie's dark eyes. "That sweater that he kept!" she exclaimed, her lip trembling.

Maida put her arms about Rosie. "Think how happy it made his mother to know that he kept it," she said.

Rosie's quick smile succeeded her swift tears. "I know it did," she said, and added, "I'm knitting a new sweater, dark blue, for Mrs. Morgan. Bunny's helping me."

"Anyway," Maida said, "Mrs. Morgan has had a month's rest and vacation. She's a different-looking woman."

"She certainly is," Silva commented. "Nothing could make her eyes brighter—they're so big and shining. But she's grown a little plumper and there's pink in her cheeks."

"I've noticed," Maida agreed briefly. "I wish—" But Maida did not say what she wished, and the girls would not ask her about it.

Not once had Maida mentioned her father's name,

but that night she wrote him a letter. It was blotted, much crossed out, much written over and very, very long.

After two days, an answer came from Mr. Westabrook. He said:

My dear little daughter,

Don't trouble your loving head with all these matters. Everything you've been thinking I've been thinking too. Everything is coming out all right, I'm sure.

Your devoted Dad.

But days went by and nothing happened. And then one day, Maida heard Mrs. Morgan on the telephone. She was talking to Mr. Westabrook. "The six weeks of your invitation are up, Monday, Mr. Westabrook," she was saying, "and I want you to know that I'm getting ready to go back to Boston that day. I can't thank you enough. At least, I don't know how to thank you enough. But my heart is full of gratitude, not alone for what you have done for me, but for what you've done for Bliss. I can never pay you back, but I wish you could think of something I could do for you. I'd work my fingers to the bone."

What her father answered, Maida did not, of course, hear.

"I believe miracles can happen," Maida said to the other girls that night, when they went to bed. Maida's eyes were shining with happiness. For something that seemed a miracle had occurred at the Little House that afternoon.

Mr. Westabrook had come for luncheon. And afterwards all the household, Granny Flynn, Mrs. Dore, Mrs. Morgan, Bunny, Robin and the Big Ten, sat on the lawn talking.

Suddenly a man's figure appeared on the road. "Here's Mr. Maybury!" Rosie exclaimed. "Goodness, I hope King Solomon hasn't got loose again!"

Everyone laughed. Then they saw that Mr. Maybury's face, usually so gay, looked troubled.

"Come up and take a seat, Mart," Mr. Westabrook called. "Now what's on your mind?" he demanded as Mr. Maybury, with a groan of relaxation, leaned back in the lawn chair.

"I've got trouble, Mr. Westabrook," Mart Maybury said. "This morning when I woke up, there was no sound from the kitchen. Myra wasn't there. I went to her room and knocked and called. Nobody answered. After a while, I opened the door. Myra wasn't there. What's more, there wasn't a dud of hers in the room or in the closet. I paid her her week's salary last night, and she must have vamoosed in the night. I don't know how she did it. She must have packed her suitcase in the afternoon and taken it down the road and hid it in the bushes. Then, late, after we were all asleep, someone must have come in a car, and she lighted out."

"I'm glad she's gone," Rosie declared. "I think she

was the most disagreeable girl I ever saw, and Flora-bel and Poppy and Della say the same. If I never see her again, it will be too soon!"

A general laugh followed this explosion. Mr. May-bury laughed more heartily than anyone, and the lines of trouble vanished from his face. All its gay good nature came back.

"Well, it occurred to me," he went on. "To tell you the truth, it occurred to Elvira first—she's al-ways so quick on the trigger—that maybe Mrs. Morgan would be willing to help us out. Elvira took an awful shine to you, Mrs. Morgan. You'd have a nice big room, with your own bath, and the work isn't hard. Before you say a word, Mrs. Morgan, I want to add that your boy could live with us, too. There's a nice little room right beside yours. He could help with the chores." He paused to smile. "You could take care of King Solomon, Scrab."

"Oh, mother," Scrab cried, "say yes! say yes! We'll be right next to the Little House and we'll live in the country all the year round—like you told me so many times you'd love to. And I can skate on the Magic Mirror!"

"Hold your horses, Scrab!" Mr. Maybury said. "There are other things your mother'd want to set-tle first—like salary, for instance."

"Bunny and I will take the rest of the Big Ten up the road for a walk," Robin declared. "We'll be gone —shall we say a half an hour, Mart? Is that long enough?"

"Fifteen minutes will be plenty," Mart Maybury answered.

"I'd say five," Mrs. Morgan faltered.

When Robin's expedition returned, Scrab met it with an ecstatic somersault. "It's all settled!" he cried jubilantly. "We're going to move to the farm tomorrow morning. Mr. Maybury said he wanted to get someone in today to clean our rooms first. I couldn't see that there was anything that needed cleaning up, but Miss Elvira said boys never can see dirt. Oh, what a fine room my mother's got! Two big windows—"

"Looking out on the cows at pasture," Mrs. Morgan interrupted, "and the sunset. I'll see the full moon rise, too."

"And there's a cabinet in my room," Scrab boasted. "Mr. Maybury said it was a secretary-desk. I can keep my stamp book in it, and all the things you gave me for my birthday, and my harmonica."

"We promised to leave the great surprise to the end," Mr. Westabrook said. "Go ahead, Mrs. Morgan. Tell them."

"Midge is coming to the farm, too—that is, if she would like to," Mrs. Morgan said. "Her room will be on one side of mine and Bliss's on the other." She paused and smiled at the wide-eyed little girl. "And Midge dear, I—I'd love it if you'd call me mother."

"That makes Midge practically my sister," Scrab claimed. "Gee, I'm glad to have a sister. I wish I had a brother too."

"Perhaps we'll find a brother for you, one day," Mr. Westabrook said.

"I wouldn't be surprised, Mr. Westabrook," Scrab answered. "I see that almost anything can happen in the Little House."

"And Miss Elvira said," Mrs. Morgan concluded the story, "how happy she'd be to have two children in the house. She said she would be so grateful if Midge would do her errands for her, and help her to dress, and wheel her where she wanted to go. And she said that tomorrow night, she'd start reading *Little Women* to Midge. And after that, she'll read *Little Men* and after that *Jo's Boys*. Won't that be fun? Miss Elvira says she hasn't read them for years and she's crazy to read them again."

Midge's face was so full of happiness that light seemed to splash from her wide excited eyes. "You mustn't think that I want to leave the Little House. I don't. But I thought I would have to go back to the Home. It seemed to me that I couldn't stand that. And now to live on a farm, almost next door to the Little House—"

"So close to that sweet, darling bull!" Rosie put in mischievously.

"I'm even going to like King Solomon," Midge admitted.

"Well, this certainly calls for a celebration!" Mr. Westabrook said.

"Then you'll stay for supper, father!" Maida caught him up quickly.

"I will on condition that Rosie cooks me some baked apples," Mr. Westabrook bargained.

"I *will* cook you some baked apples, Mr. Westabrook," Rosie agreed, "and I guess I'd better get about it at once."

"Father," Maida said in a low voice to her father, "when did you cook this up with Miss Elvira?"

Mr. Westabrook scowled at his daughter, smiled at her, patted her shoulder. But he did not answer her question then, or ever.

The whole crowd dissolved and flowed into the house. There they set about various duties. Mrs. Morgan, assisted by Scrab, began to pack.

"Where'd you get that suitcase, mom?" Scrab asked, his eyes as big as saucers. "Gee, isn't it nice! And your initials, J. M., on both ends!"

"Mr. Westabrook gave it to me," Mrs. Morgan replied. Her voice was muffled, for she was deep in the capacious closet, bending over something. She came out into the room with another suitcase in her hand exactly the same size and color as hers. She held it endwise out to Scrab.

"How do you like that?" she asked gaily.

On the end were the initials, B. M.

"Is it really mine, mom?" Scrab gasped. "Did Mr. Westabrook buy it for me?"

"The same time he bought mine," his mother nodded. "It's airplane luggage. That's why it's so light."

Scrab lifted both suitcases and hefted them. "What

do you know!" he exclaimed. "Mom, when I'm earning money, I'm going to try to pay Mr. Westabrook back. Of course there's nothing we could buy him," he ended sadly. "He has everything he wants. But maybe there's something I can *do* for him."

"We'll find something to do," his mother assured him, "but I've got to think about it."

There came a knock at the door. "Come in!" Mrs. Morgan said.

Rosie entered. She was carrying a flat box. "Here's something I made for you, Mrs. Morgan," she said. "At least, I did the knitting. Bunny had to tell me how to do everything. I hope you'll like it."

"You blessed child!" Mrs. Morgan exclaimed. She sat down on the bed and opened the box. Inside, folded in white tissue paper, was a dark blue woolen cardigan sweater. "Oh!" Mrs. Morgan exclaimed. "What a beautiful piece of work, and what a lovely color, and how warm! And what nice dark blue buttons!" Arising and standing before the mirror of her dressing table, she slipped on the cardigan. "It fits perfectly!" she exclaimed. "Oh, how I shall enjoy it! You darling little girl!" She kissed Rosie.

"Mom," Scrab exclaimed after Rosie had left, "that was a swell thing for Rosie to do. Maybe," he added wistfully, "I can do something for her some time. There are so many people I'd like to do something for. Jiminy, I've got to learn how to make things. All the boys here can make things."

In the meantime, the Little House resounded with the scurrying of busy feet. Rosie went at once to the kitchen to bake apples for Mr. Westabrook. Maida and Silva, as was always their custom in the case of company, enlarged the dining-room table and set it. The sun was dropping to the horizon in a red glow, but a crisp, sharp wind had come up. The boys of the Big Ten laid a fire in the living room, brought in extra wood.

Mr. Westabrook had gone into the hall, where he made two telephone calls. One message was to the Big House, not to expect him for dinner. The other was to a shop in the town of Satuit.

They sat down to delicious broiled ham, baked sweet potatoes, stewed tomatoes, Rosie's baked apples and hot biscuits. The dessert proved to be what Mr. Westabrook had ordered from Satuit—a dessert that the Big Eight had never before tasted—frozen pudding. It was ice cream loaded with fruit. Fortunately, Mr. Westabrook knew children well enough to order twice as much as an inexperienced person would expect them to eat.

After supper, the boys arranged the chairs in a big semicircle about the fireplace. Arthur touched a match to the piled wood and suddenly the whole room took on a rosy glow.

"Oh, let's put out the lights!" Bunny exclaimed. "The firelight is so beautiful."

The boys obeyed her. Instantly the semicircle seemed to be half in shadow and half in the light of a great luminous rose that burned in the fireplace.

They talked about all kinds of things, from the frozen pudding to King Solomon.

Suddenly Maida exclaimed, "There's a picture in the fire. It makes me think of our scow, our houseboat —the Ark. Oh, do you remember," she went on, "when we suddenly discovered that the scow had pulled away from its moorings and we were afloat in the midst of a terrible storm—somewhere in Massachusetts Bay? We were frightened," she ended, "and we prayed."

"And the first thing we knew," Dicky put in, "the Ark had grounded on Spectacles, and we were all safe."

"Let's pretend there's another picture in the fire," Silva suggested, "Oh, I know—our little theater that we named after Shakespeare's theater, the Globe. What fun it was, rehearsing! Robin asked me to design the curtain, but when it came to the painting of it, you all helped. Do you remember, there was a map on it. On the west was Massachusetts with one town on it—Satuit. And on the east was England with one city on it—London. And all the Atlantic Ocean between them! Oh, how I enjoyed doing that!"

"I'm pretending to see another picture," Arthur added. "Our zoo."

"Oh!" all the rest of the Big Eight groaned, "the zoo! What fun we had that year!"

"Tell mom and Midge and me about the zoo," Scrab begged.

"Well, a friend of my father's" Maida began it, "has a private zoo on his place. He was going away for the summer and he offered to lend us the zoo."

"Lend the zoo!" Scrab exclaimed. "How can you lend a zoo?"

"That's what we thought," Arthur answered him. "But first they sent the animals' houses here and then they sent the animals. The zoo was open all summer long to anyone who wanted to visit it."

The Big Eight went on recalling happy days, and the grownups listened in silence.

But there was one picture that the fire might have shown them. Only it had not happened yet. How the people in the Little House would have enjoyed it!

In that picture, Mrs. Morgan had become Mrs. Martin Maybury. In that picture, Martin Maybury had legally adopted both Midge and Scrab. In that picture there was daily communication between the Maybury farm and the Little House. Granny Flynn and Mrs. Dore were constantly calling on Mrs. Morgan, now Mrs. Maybury, and Mrs. Maybury was constantly calling on them. Scrab and Midge were constantly appearing at the Little House to go swimming in the summer, skating in the winter, and for picnics on Spectacles.

Promptly at half-past nine, Mr. Westabrook departed and everyone in the Little House went to bed.

But in the warm living room, the little flames on the dying embers kept up a gentle persistent whisper, as though the fire were still trying to describe that last picture.

Maida's Little Shop
Primrose Court
Massachusetts
House Rock
Sand
The Magic Mirror
Fairy Ring
Tree House
Road to Maida's Little Camp in the Adirondacks
The Little House
The Big House
The Stonecrop
Tilestone Hollow
Boy's House
Mess Hall
Girl's House
Old Mill
MILL ROAD
Tilestone Lane
Post Office
Brick House
The Barn